My Heart Belongs to Teaching

JOANN TRYLOFF

Copyright © 2017 JoAnn Tryloff
All rights reserved
First Edition

Cover Design by Samantha Witte
Photo by Roger Garrell

PAGE PUBLISHING, INC.
New York, NY

First originally published by Page Publishing, Inc. 2017

ISBN 978-1-64082-331-0 (Paperback)
ISBN 978-1-64082-332-7 (Digital)

Printed in the United States of America

Contents

1. The Truth According to a Child 17
2. Never Again 24
3. The Hyper Kid 30
4. Embarrassing Moments 33
5. Caught You! 41
6. Field Trips 46
7. Fads—They Come and Go 52
8. Holidays 56
9. Play on Words 65
10. Picture Day 72
11. Simply Said 75
12. Talent 80
13. Out of the Mouth of Babes 82
14. Above and Beyond the Call of Duty 89
15. So Brave, So Sad 94
16. Kisses and Puppy Love 102
17. Reading 108
18. Random Acts of Kindness 111
19. It Was All Worth It 115
20. Looking Back—It Was Wonderful! 121

This book is dedicated to all the children whose lives I have touched over the years. I hope I've enriched their lives as much as they have enriched mine.

Praise for JoAnn Tryloff

"Laugh, cry, and just enjoy the stories. For any future teacher, this is a must read. This book is filled with several different stories that have *actually* happened in real life, and just might as well happen in your future classroom. Mrs. Tryloff has opened up her past classrooms for our enjoyment and there is so much to learn from her adventures with her students, their parents, and the faculty and staff of her school."

Allison Goodwin
—Student, Duquesne University, Pennsylvania

"Reading JoAnn's book was a great experience. Most of the stories cause one to smile, giggle, or even laugh out loud. However, some cause sadness, perhaps even tears. Many times, I stopped to walk down my own memory land—to remember incidents that happened when I, too, was in a classroom. You don't have to be old enough to remember Art Linkletter to enjoy JoAnn's book."

Bonnie Robb
—Elementary teacher, Fitzgerald School, Warren, Michigan

"Stories signify the author's love of . . .

Tremendous
Enjoyable
Awesome
Clever
Heart-Warming
Interesting
Nice
Great"

Marel Bolger Staisil
—Teacher/Administrator, Flint Community Schools, Michigan

Special Thanks

A thousand thanks to my patient husband for encouraging me to complete this book and believing it is special enough to publish.

Special thanks to my great friends Katie Sharp and Roger Garrell for all their encouragement during the writing process. Katie helped organize my stories and did all the typing.

Thanks to my wonderful friends Marel Staisil, Bonnie Schmidt, and Allison Goodwin for taking the time to proofread and critique my book.

Recommendation

This book would be a great gift to someone who enjoys children or to a student considering a teaching profession. Teachers, parents, and grandparents will get a giggle out of this book and will really relate. A fun read to relax you after a stressful day at work.

Introduction

Many years ago, I had the joy of teaching delightful, young children. This book contains the "good moments" of teaching, the special, little things that tug on your heart and push you to go back year after year. This book makes you realize teaching is such a satisfying career. As much as you give to the profession you get back ten times over.

The brightest people I've seen in relation to accepting new ideas are five- to eight-year-olds. They are open minded and more than ready to try anything new. At this early age, they aren't afraid of failure–if something doesn't work out, they don't quit. They keep trying to do it again and again, each time approaching the problem just a little differently until it is solved. Science experiments are so much fun to do with this age group.

Early primary children have such a sense of adventure. I thoroughly enjoyed being around them. This book is about what children in kindergarten through third grade are doing out there in their bright and promising world.

Yes, I know. You could have easily written this book. Anyone who is around children–parents, teachers, scout leaders, school bus drivers, and coaches will read this book and think, "I've heard those exact words before." Or "I've seen a kid act exactly like that." Or "My gosh! That's my Jimmy exactly. He did the same thing."

All these incidents really happened. Nothing has been made up. Not all have happened to me. My friends have shared some of their best "kid stories" with me. The names have been changed to protect the innocent, and more often, the guilty.

Read and enjoy. Laugh, giggle, and share with your family and friends.

"Imagination is more important than knowledge."
—Albert Einstein

"I agree!" (JoAnn Tryloff).

September

September! The beginning of another school year. The children bounced into my classroom, exuberance shining in their bright eyes. They were full of life, kindness, anxiousness, wiggles, capriciousness, aggression, compassion, generosity, resilience, and resistance. Could I possibly direct all this nervous energy toward learning? I was filled with the wonder of a new class, the anticipation of each day, each season and holiday, each challenge and success, the mystery and surprise as each child grew and developed. Teaching was never a job to me. It was always a joy! I was so lucky to be able to do the work I enjoyed, to be with the people I loved, and to be happy to come to work each day.

Share These Stories

Children don't always have to hear stories about talking animals or read about the perfect kid who has a problem which is easily solved in a three-page story. They really enjoy hearing about regular kids just like themselves. Kids who get into real trouble or do foolish and embarrassing things. They love to hear about these types of things that happened to their parents and teachers and what kind of trouble they got into when they were the same age.

If you're a parent or teacher, please read some of these stories to your children. You can tell them these stories actually happened to real children their same age. I've put a ☺ in the corner of the stories I think are appropriate for a child. And I bet they'll sneak a peek sometimes when you're gone to read some of the stories you've skipped.

Enjoy!

Chapter 1

The Truth According to a Child

Pickup Sticks ☺

    In kindergarten, I would often show my children how to play old-fashioned, simple games like jacks, hopscotch, and dominos. One summer, I found a game of pickup sticks at a garage sale. That fall, I started to show the children how to play it.

    "First you drop the sticks on the floor. Then very carefully, you try to pick them up, one by one . . ."

    Before I could finish, I heard Ron whisper to Dave, "Heck, I'd just go get the vacuum cleaner."

Really Tiny ☺

    As Danny was looking at Alice's baby sister, he commented, "My Grandpa said I was even smaller than your sister. He said I was once knee-high to a grasshopper."

Saved by the Phone ☺

After hearing the story about Hansel and Gretel, where the children dropped pieces of bread to leave a trail to follow back home, Adam said, "They wouldn't have gotten in all that trouble if they brought their cell phones."

Hat Trick

Brandon and Andrew were playing shoot 'em up cowboys in the corner. Brandon offered Andrew a bit of advice. "You always got to wear a black hat. If you have a white one on, you'll have to kiss a girl. I found that out by watching lots of cowboy movies."

Only a Stick ☺

Our grade school collected nickels and dimes for three months to buy something special for our school's twenty-fifth anniversary. The children voted to buy a tree and plant it near the front door of the school.

As one of the fifth graders was planting the small stick-like tree into the ground, Brian whispered to Roger, "I wish we would've had more money. Then we could've bought some leaves, too."

Where's The Older Kids? ☺

As the kindergarten children were lining up to go home after their first day of school, Paul tugged on my skirt.

"Mrs. Tryloff, why are all these kids five years old? Where are the all the older kids?"

Before I could figure out what he was talking about, he added, "All last year my mom said, 'Next year you'll get to go to school with the older kids.'"

I smiled and said, "Guess what, Paul. You're the older kid now. The three- and four-year-olds are just waiting to get into our class."

Paul went home beaming.

Where Are the Lines? ☺

The kindergarten class had carefully colored in a tree trunk near the bottom of their paper and were wildly scribbling in leaves across the top using the special fall-colored crayons we'd picked out. Meanwhile, Andy just sat there paralyzed.

When I asked if he needed some help, he replied, "Where are the lines? My mom said it's good art only when you stay in the lines."

Wash Your Hands ☺

We were getting ready for our Christmas party and the kindergarten children were passing out the treats that their mothers sent to school. As each table had their bathroom break, I asked them to wash their hands carefully because we were going to eat soon. Peter whispered to Pam, "I only have to wash one hand. I'm right-handed, you know."

Younger Brothers and Sisters ☺

I enjoyed hearing children talk about their younger brothers and sisters.

Jamie told me her year-old brother was talking a mile a minute before the bus came to pick her up. "But Mrs. Tryloff, I couldn't understand him because I don't speak his language."

Emily was writing about her brother, Michael, who was in kindergarten, and she wrote the following: I have a little brother named Michael who really gets on my nerves all the time, but I'm training him to be a decent person.

Family Lie ☺

We were talking about being honest and telling the truth even though it might cause trouble for you. Honest Debra raised her hand and announced, "When my grandma Anderson calls, my mother runs out the back door to give the dog some water. Then I can say, 'Mom just went out for a while and she'll call you back after supper.' And that's not even a white lie, it's the truth."

Old Movies ☺

Before Easter, I was showing the class an old Peter Rabbit movie from the 1950s. I told my kids it was one of my favorite movies when I was their age. I heard Alice say to Brandy, "When movies get old, they lose their color and turn black and white."

100% ☺

As I passed out our final spelling tests, I overheard James tell his friend, "Darn, I only got an 82. At least I had 100 when my mother took my temperature two nights ago."

Peas Please ☺

We'd been working on a food unit and I had the children practice their table manners at the same time. The week after, Aimee's mother stopped in to tell me that the good manners lesson was a success. She said she had her boss over for dinner and told her three children to be on their best behavior. They weren't supposed to whine about the food, leave the table without being excused, start giggling, etc. They had to take a small amount of everything served and clean their plates.

Aimee's mother served peas which she realized Aimee detested. When the peas were passed to Aimee, she said, "Peas! I just love them! I'll have two please. Thank you."

Everyone tried very hard to hold back their laughter.

Nerds versus the Oks ☺

Third graders start forming cliques and can really be mean to the "outsiders."

One afternoon, the children came in after lunch and settled down to their creative writing assignment. A few of the girls and boys were passing a yellow notepad around and writing on it as each row went out for their bathroom break. I let it continue because they weren't causing a disturbance. Ten minutes later, sensitive Cindy came up and said, "Mrs. Tryloff, Sheila is writing bad things about me."

I asked to see what they were writing. I was handed a chart the group had started to make up during lunch time.

NERDS	OKS
John	Billy P
William	Sheila
Jean	Bonnie
Kathy	James
Bob	

I brought the five children who were writing the chart to my desk and said they were hurting the feelings of the rest of their classmates. "No we're not," said Sheila. "We're only showing the chart to the Oks."

JOANN TRYLOFF

Mind on Vacation ☺

I'd just handed back our first spelling test of the year. Pat had gotten a "C" and I could tell he was very disappointed. I heard him whisper to Doug, "My body is back from summer vacation, but it looks like my brain won't be back for a few weeks."

Nationality?

In social studies, we were discussing where our ancestors came from. The children were raising their hands and telling me they knew they were Irish, Polish, Italian, etc. Andrew raised his hand and when called on he said uncertainly, "I don't know for sure, but I think I'm Catholic."

Homework Excuses

Over the years, I've heard all the excuses including, "The dog ate my homework." I've received a few papers that the dog did try to eat, and I actually almost believed this excuse. Also, "The baby ate my homework" is another excuse I've often heard. The excuses were funny, sad, silly, pitiful, and often true.

One clever boy named John, when asked about his missing homework, said, "My mother told me I had to rest my brain so I'd be sharp for today's science test."

I've also had homework flushed down the toilet. "Why did you do your homework in the bathroom?" I asked. "Because my sister was bugging me."

Often I heard, "I just didn't have time. I went home, ate dinner, and then my mother made me to go bed."

Sometimes its scouts, church, a rented video, or a pro basketball game on TV that interferes with the children doing their homework.

One morning, Jim said he didn't get his homework done because he had a fire in his trailer. I was just about to make a sarcastic remark about not believing him when Pete said, "Hey Jim, I saw your place on the way to school. Where are you going to live now?" I felt so ashamed!

An age-old excuse is, "It blew out of my hand and a car or bus ran over it."

I've had many children hide their assignments so their parents wouldn't be aware they had homework that night. I never handed out homework until we were leaving for the day. No one could get out of their seats until I'd checked to see if their page of homework was dated and had their name on it. After the children left, I found homework in other kid's desks and in the wastebaskets. Children from different classes brought in homework sheets that had been buried under snow or hidden in the bushes around the school. Parents have found homework under mattresses, in their children's sock drawer and in the basement with Christmas ornaments.

On the other hand, many children were very conscientious. Some students who'd left their homework in the room ran back to school in tears to check their desks. If the room was locked, they went to the office to get a janitor to open the room. A few even called a friend when they couldn't find their homework. They'd copy down all the math problems or science questions to be sure they had their homework completed by the next morning. Teaching wasn't always a battle. It often was very rewarding!

Chapter 2

Never Again

International Food Festival

My friend Jean, who taught the other kindergarten class, was always thinking of new ideas to try. She'd get bored doing things the same old way. Of course, I'd always go along with her schemes, often adding other ideas to the project. It never hurt to try, and if they didn't work out, we just didn't try them again.

I was really hesitant when Jean got all excited about having an international food festival. It sounded like an awful lot of work, but I thought it could be fun. We had children of all nationalities in our classes that year, so each child was asked to bring in a food that their grandparents enjoyed. We were lucky to be able to use an oven in our special education room while that class was on a field trip.

The morning started pretty calmly. Some wonderful mothers brought in trays of food cut into twenty-eight bite-sized pieces. After teaching for forty-five minutes, we took both classes down to the "Food Fest" room and started warming up the dishes that needed to be served hot. We realized we had problems: 350° for ten minutes; 400° for twenty minutes; 325° for one hour, 425° for fifteen minutes, then reduce heat to 375° for ten minutes, etc.!

We turned the oven to 400° and just layered the pans four deep on each shelf. Food started spilling and leaking out of their pans, and smoke poured out of the oven.

More mothers came in with even more dishes! Some would just hand us a large, cold kielbasa with thick skin and then leave. Some children informed us, "We've got out food in our backpacks back in the classroom. We forgot to give it to you." We seemed to have so much food! It kept multiplying!

Fifty-four children were tasting little bits of strange foods. We told them if they didn't like it after the first bite, they could throw it away in one of the two garbage cans at each end of the room. Such waste! Five-year-olds don't eat much–especially strange, spicy foods. We were going crazy keeping the kids from burning themselves on pans, while cutting giant casseroles into small bites. Food and drinks were spilling everywhere and our shoes were sticking to the floor as we raced from the smoking oven to the large tables to help the children.

One girl got sick, which caused about ten children to stop eating immediately. We sent two children to get more garbage bags and a mop and pail. We also sent a note to the sixth grade for two children to come help out. More mothers arrived about a half hour before the children were going home. Several of them decided everything looked so good that they just plopped down and helped themselves to the food. "We won't have to fix lunch today," they said.

Jean and I couldn't believe it! Couldn't they see we needed help to clean up for the afternoon class!

Overall, the children were very well-behaved and the mothers that helped were great. We were exhausted by 11:30 a.m., but kept right on working. We washed tables, scraped the gook off the stove, stored food in foil, all during lunch hour. Then, we had to repeat the "Food Fest" for the afternoon class! Our backs were killing us. We were greasy, smelly, and food-stained, but we survived.

I decided if two or more children brought kielbasa, I'd just cook one and tell the others it was their sausage. We also decided that any food that was delivered late wouldn't be served unless the mother stayed to help.

As the children left for home, we tried hard to stuff leftover food into their backpacks. Most wouldn't take it. They'd say, "We don't like that. My mother just made it for the festival."

At 3:00 p.m., we were left with tons of food and one sticky, stinky room. Any teacher who peeked in to see if we'd survived got a care package of food to take home. Our principal had six children, so we wheeled all kinds of casseroles and platters to his office. I'm sure his wife didn't have to cook for three days.

Once we got the food distributed, we cleaned the room as best we could. We couldn't let Mary see what we'd done to her special education room!

Afterwards, Jean admitted, "Never again! This was stupid! We're totally nuts!"

I more than agreed. But, our school talked about that International Food Festival the rest of the year. They loved it!

Licked Too Quick ☺

The class was busy getting ready for our annual Mother's Day program. I was making costumes, helping the children with their lines, and preparing invitations for the class to take home. Samantha knew I was very busy and asked if she could help me.

I handed her sixty envelopes from my desk and pointed to the invitations piled on the table behind me. "Pick a friend and the two of you can get these envelopes ready to go home."

Fifteen minutes later, the two girls proudly brought the envelopes to me.

Samantha said, "We licked all the envelopes, Mrs. Tryloff."

My heart sank as I realized the envelopes were looking very skinny. You guessed it! They were having so much fun licking the envelopes, they forgot to put the invitations inside.

M&M's

I love peanut M&M's. Just for fun one year, I decided to brainwash my children with hints to see if they would give me any peanut M&M's for a gift. I'd mention about once a week that when I got home, I was going to have my favorite snack–peanut M&M's. I'd eat lunch at my desk and leave an M&M wrapper on top of my desk. If some child brought in M&M'S for a treat, I'd be sure to ask for extras because I loved them soooo much. As Christmas approached, I thought for sure I'd get lots of M&M treats. I figured at least a few children would have been indoctrinated.

As I opened each of my wonderful gifts, I waited and waited. There wasn't one single package of peanut M&M's. I couldn't believe it. Did the mothers buy the teacher's gift without consulting with their children? "Oh well," I thought, "I'd just have to keep buying my own."

Two years later, my teacher friend in the fourth grade tried the same thing with her class. Christmas arrived and she got lots of M&M's. One sweet boy gave her a Christmas cup with three packages of M&M's: plain, peanut, and almond. He said he couldn't remember which ones she liked best. I guess I just wasn't persuasive enough with my class!

Cafeteria Catastrophe ☺

First grade can be just as traumatic as kindergarten. Children have to stay at school a full day for the first time. They get tired in the afternoon, and early in the school year, some actually fall asleep right at their desks. They don't get any play time except recess, and they have to sit quietly for sooooo long and do a lot of school work.

Then there is lunchtime. Some children are afraid to even stay and eat lunch in the cafeteria. They continue to walk home and eat with Mommy. Some don't like the strange food that's put on their tray and they hate to wait in line to get their food, so they bring a packed lunch with familiar peanut butter and jelly sandwiches, cookies, and little bags of chips.

Marilyn was quite shy and afraid she wouldn't know what to do in the large, noisy, busy cafeteria, so she always went home for lunch. One day, her mom had a doctor's appointment and told Marilyn she would have to buy her lunch that day. All morning, Marilyn worried about going to the cafeteria and what the procedure would be.

When the children started to get their coats and lunches, she quickly checked to see if she still had her quarter tied in a hankie. She got it out and held it tightly in her hand. Then, because she was stressed, she had to use the bathroom before she left for lunch. As she reached down to pull up her pants, she accidentally dropped the quarter into the toilet. Now she was panicked. No money for lunch, stuck in the bathroom, and everyone leaving to walk to the lunch room with the teacher.

Ten minutes later, when I got back to the room, I heard someone crying in the bathroom area. I discovered poor, miserable Marilyn. I quickly got our small fish net from our fish tank and started fishing for Marilyn's quarter. Thank heavens she hadn't flushed it! I washed it off for her and she gingerly clutched it in her hand again. Then off to the cafeteria she went.

Of course, Marilyn was late and had to get in line with an older class. She was so upset she thought everyone was looking at her when we walked in together, and I'm sure she figured they somehow knew how dumb she'd been to drop her quarter into the stinky toilet. By the time she took her tray to the first grade table, most of the other children were done eating and had left for the playground and she had to eat alone.

Marilyn never used the cafeteria again that year.

Brain and Brawn Day

Our principal had a great idea! Brain and Brawn Day! One spring day, we were going to have team contests. Each class would be divided into two teams wearing different colors. There would be lots of prizes. Half the day would be devoted to contests of the brain—experiments, puzzles, and word games. The other half of the day we'd have brawn contests—sports and games outside. He asked each child to bring in a white t-shirt so the art teacher could dye them in their team colors.

Poor Jane, our art teacher—350 T-shirts to dye! First, there was the problem of the children remembering to bring in a t-shirt. Then there was the monumental task of dying them two different colors. Jane worked all afternoon and all night. Brain and Brawn Day arrived and she was still at the laundromat trying to dry the last shirts. With no time left, she just brought the damp shirts to school and spread them out on our library tables to dry. Of course, there were no names on the shirts. Each class walked through the library and tried to find a shirt that would fit and was the right color.

My poor second grade class was last to select their shirts. They ended up with shirts that were either too large or too small–plus still quite damp. The children were disappointed and started to grumble. When we got back to the room, we opened the windows and draped the damp shirts over the window ledges.

Ten minutes after we'd started class, we were called outside for the Brawn part of the competition. It was quite cool out and I said we couldn't wear our shirts because they were still damp. Children started pouting, crying, and a few said they weren't going outside without their shirts on their backs. What a mess! I quickly pinned paper strips of color on their jackets and off we went into the cold morning air for the Brawn games.

In the afternoon, we did put our shirts on for the brain games. It was a fun day, but needless to say, we never had another Brain and Brawn Day!

Chapter 3

The Hyper Kid

Ritalin: Not Always the Answer

Dave's mother was desperate! She couldn't keep up with Dave's moods, constant movement, and disruptive activities. He was constantly yelling, screaming, running, hitting, and totally unable to settle down and focus on anything in our kindergarten room. He was making my life difficult, too.

We got counselors, doctors, and special education teachers to work with him. One doctor thought the "magic drug" Ritalin would be the answer. Dave tried it for a few months but it didn't slow him down a bit. Finally, after about six months, the solution for Dave's mother was a prescription for herself so she could put up with Dave. As for me and my class, we continued to suffer through Dave's disruptions. By fourth grade, Dave had finally started to settle down.

Special Seat

George was a likeable, but hyper and easily distracted, child. I had him in kindergarten and now he was in first grade. His teacher couldn't keep him focused on his work even though he was quite bright.

We had just given a play in which we'd used a giant refrigerator box for the gingerbread house. Mrs. Smith, George's teacher, had an idea. She asked for the box, cut it into a special work station and put it in the back corner of the room so George could concentrate. He basically was isolated from the rest of the hustle of the classroom. The idea was, if he could get his lessons done, he could gradually work his way back to his regular seat and be with his friends again.

When George and his mother came to my kindergarten open house to see his sister's work, George kept saying to his mother, "I want you to see my special seat in Mrs. Smith's room."

George was just beaming he was so excited. I thought, "Oh no! He's proud of it. He doesn't ever want to leave his little cocoon."

I was right. Mrs. Smith had made his seat so attractive it was months before George rejoined the rest of the class. So much for the best laid plans. George did eventually calm down but he always remembered his special seat with affection.

Taking No Chances

Allan was a typical ADD (attention deficit disorder) child. He had a very short attention span and was always on the move. He'd already been retained a year, but I felt his IQ was at least average or above. We worked with the special education teacher, his family, and his doctor and decided to try the drug, Ritalin. Allan's mother was against drugs of any kind. She was afraid they might be addictive or have side effects. After talking with the doctor, she agreed to try Ritalin on a trial basis to see if it would help.

It really did calm Allan down and his grades went up significantly in all his subjects. After Allan had been taking Ritalin for a month, we met with his mother to tell her the good results. She listened to us for a few minutes and then she admitted, "I was so worried about the medication that I took it myself for a week. I didn't feel any different so I guess Allan can stay on it."

In a Rut

Jamie was a hell-on-wheels guy. He never stopped! Just talk, talk, talk, run, push, shove, wiggle, and bother his friends. Yet everyone liked him, even his teachers. He didn't have a mean bone in his body. Jamie was constantly in motion and just couldn't stop himself.

It was shortly after Easter, the last stretch until summer. My kids were all getting antsy. I made a chart over the weekend and each day the children were well-behaved, they got a star. At the end of the week, if they had a star for each day, they got to choose a prize from the prize box. It was working wonders, except with Jamie.

A month went by and everyone had earned at least one prize, except Jamie. The next week, I was handing out the prizes during last hour on Friday. Lo and behold, Jamie had earned a chance to pick out a prize! His classmates all clapped as he came up to the prize box. He looked surprised, but pleased. I'm sure he was amazed that he was capable of being good for so long.

As the children were getting ready to go home, I overheard Adam congratulate him. "Boy Jamie, you finally got a neat prize."

Jamie still looked stunned and said, "I guess I got in a rut or something. I was good for a whole week. Wait 'til my Mom hears this!"

Chapter 4

Embarrassing Moments

Right Street, Wrong President

I was so excited! I had received a call from my college three days earlier changing my student teaching assignment. I would be able to live at home and the new school was only forty minutes away.

I arrived early at George Washington Elementary School and introduced myself to the principal as the new student teacher for second grade. She gave me a strange look and said, "We aren't having a student teacher this semester."

I was devastated!

"Just wait a few minutes," she said. "I'll call around and see what I can find out."

She soon came back with a smile on her face. "You're expected at Thomas Jefferson Elementary." She gave me directions and I hurried over to the school, which was on the same street, less than a mile away. I hadn't even looked at the address. In my excitement, I'd just stopped at the first school I saw on that street. Wrong president–wrong school. Late and embarrassed, I finally arrived at the correct school. What a great way to start my teaching career!

Homeward Bound ☺

I'll never forget taking my kindergarten children out for recess during the first week of school. I was pushing Janice on the swings when Todd ran up to me and said, "Tony and some of the kids are walking home."

Sure enough, I spotted them crossing our bus driveway and heading off the school property. They were too far away for them to hear me, so I had to send someone in to the office since I couldn't leave the other children alone. Our principal hopped into his car, picked them up, and brought them back to school. I was so embarrassed! Once they had their coats on, they automatically assumed they were heading home for the day.

Flat Tryloff

One of the first stories we covered in reading every year was *Flat Stanley*. The children loved how Stanley got flattened out and all the crazy things he could do because he was flat. As an extra activity, each of the children made a page for a class book of things that are flat. They drew and colored the objects and then wrote about them under the picture.

As I was putting the book together, I smiled as I read some of their pages:

"A cat is flat sometimes." There was a picture of a car running over a cat.

"The world is flat. That's what they used to say." The picture showed a ship falling off the edge of the ocean.

Then there were more normal things like a ruler is flat, my desk is flat, our flag is flat, a birthday card is flat.

All of a sudden, I came to a page that had a great picture of me saying "Mrs. Tryloff is flat." I cracked up and had to show all my friends and husband. I hoped Sheila was referring to the fact that I am tall and thin.

Out of my Sight

Tim had been on a rampage since he stepped into the classroom: mean, sulking, loud, and challenging. He must have gotten up on the wrong side of the bed or had some problems at home.

After about an hour and a half, he got so mad at his friend, Bob, that he threw a book at him, hitting Bob very near his eye and breaking the skin. As I pointed to the hall, I said, "Tim, I've had it today. Get out of here. I need some time away from you. Please just get out."

Tim pouted and left the room, slamming the door behind him.

As soon as I looked at Bob's cut and put a small bandage on it, I went out to the hall to talk to Tim. He wasn't there! Then I spied poor Tim standing outside the school entrance door hugging himself to keep warm. I quickly brought him inside and he said with tears in his eyes, "But you told me to get out."

Thank heavens I didn't say, "Get out of my sight." He might have disappeared completely!

Make a Mess, Clean It Up!

I was getting tired of some of my students walking away from their messes and letting others clean up. Before we started a pumpkin painting project, I showed the children where they could get a sponge, how to rinse it out, and how to clean the table and floor until there was no color showing. I said, "Don't worry if you knock a paint cup over. Please don't come to me and tell me some paint spilled. Just walk over here, get your sponge, and clean it up. You're responsible for your own clean up."

As I turned to help someone get started, my hip hit the corner of our easel's paint tray. Six paint cups spilled to the floor. About five children raced to get sponges to help clean the floor. True to my word, I said, "Thanks so much for bringing me sponges. You start painting our pumpkins because I must clean up this mess. I was the one who had the accident."

As the whole room worked quietly and carefully, I mopped up the mess, trying to keep my long skirt out of the paint puddle. I would have loved to have one of those eager beavers cleanup for me, but I had to practice what I preached!

Principal Slips Up

One year, we had a gruff principal who really didn't seem to relate to small children. He had just returned from a crisis in our lunchroom and was not in a good mood when he spied me standing in his office with my little trouble-maker Johnny.

He yelled, "What the hell is he in here for now?"

I meekly said, "Swearing."

He, She?

I answered the knock on my classroom door one morning in November. Our school secretary was standing there with a darling child who had just arrived from Italy two days ago. She said, "This is Micah. I hope I'm pronouncing the name right. The family can't speak English yet, but I know this kindergartener will pick it up quickly just being with your children."

Micah was a darling! All dressed up in a pastel baby blue knit pantsuit with soft leather shoes to match. She had long dark curly hair and large serious eyes with thick curly lashes. I tried to settle her in as best I could. At bathroom break, I asked Jean to show her where the girl's bathroom was. Since she was from Europe, the school hadn't received any records yet and I didn't even know how to spell her name correctly.

At the end of Micah's second day, a first grader came to our room and said he was there to walk my new boy home from school.

I said, "John, he must be in Mrs. Trent's room next door."

John looked bewildered. "No, he's in your class He just started yesterday."

"Oh my gosh," I gasped as I realized that Micah was a boy!

The next day, we showed Micah where the boy's bathroom was located. I'm sure we'd totally confused him. By the end of the week, he had picked up lots of American words. Of course, "boy" "girl" and "ok" were the first ones he learned. I often wonder if he was ever aware that for two days he was considered a girl.

I See Teacher

I was standing behind my closet door trying to pull down my blouse. I forgot there were windows on the other side. Just then I heard some of the kids who were outside for recess saying, "Look at Mrs. Tryloff's legs. I think I can see her panties."

Scissors

Scissors were an amazing attraction for children of kindergarten age. A lot of the children had never even been allowed to hold scissors, so I taught them how to hold and cut with them.

I remember I was teaching a large group how to cut off the corners of a square while Johnny was busy cutting slashes along his pant crease. As dull as their scissors were, I've seen them cut through things I could hardly believe.

I've even had some *hairy* experiences with those blunt-nosed, six inch, dull scissors.

As I was walking around the room helping the children put together a paper clown, I spotted a tuft of hair on Gary's lap. As I got closer, I found more hair that he had brushed on the floor. Gary said he was cutting the clown's hat and he leaned over to look at it and he somehow happened to cut his hair. One whole side was two or three inches shorter than the other. I called his mother before he got home to prepare her for the shock. Thank heavens she just laughed when I told her how it happened.

JOANN TRYLOFF

Mirror, Mirror on the Wall, Who Has the Fairest Hair of All?

Long ago in the same kindergarten class, there were two fair maidens with beautiful long hair. Jessica's hair was bright and shiny red while Susan's was so light in color it was almost white. It seemed everyone who entered my classroom commented on Jessica's and Susan's gorgeous hair. As the year progressed, each girl tried to be the most popular and have the most friends. They were jealous of each other, and for their age, became very catty. They never played together but each was constantly surrounded by their admirers–girls who wished they had such beautiful hair and boys who were "in love" with them.

One spring morning, I was surprised to see the two girls in the playhouse together. I felt good because it looked like they were finally getting over their jealousy and becoming friends. As I walked the children to the bus, one of the last to board was Alice who said to me, "Susan cut Jessica's hair." I glanced at Jessica through the window of the bus, but her hair looked normal.

I kept thinking of Alice's comment as I walked to the lunch room. I hurried back to my classroom and walked into the playhouse area and started looking around. I let out a scream! Hidden in the wooden oven, I found a big hunk of red hair.

No lunch for me that day! I ran to the office and called Jessica's mother. Sure enough, Jessica's hair was cut straight off on one side right below her ear. I'd seen the other side in the bus window. Jessica had told her mother Susan asked her to play beauty salon and she said, "Okay."

Jessica's mother just laughed and said she'd been wanting to cut Jessica's hair but her father loved it long. I then called Susan's mother who promised to scold Susan and make her apologize to Jessica's family. I was mortified something like could happen with those dull, blunt-nose scissors right under my nose, in the playhouse I designed so I could see into it at all times.

I Look Like Who?

We were just starting to get lined up to go home. Scott came up to me and said, "Mrs. Tryloff. You know you look just like someone in the movies."

I was thrilled! I put on my most glamorous smile and asked who he thought I looked like. "Maybe Oliva Newton-John?" I thought to myself.

Scott scratched his head and said, "Argh! I can't remember now. . . Oh, I got it! Elton John!"

Jean, my friend in the other kindergarten class, heard this exchange and just howled. The rest of the year my coworkers kept referring to me as "Elton".

Totally Embarrassing ☺

It was 9:45 a.m., the second week of school, and I was anxious for the music break because I had two calls to make to parents. As we approached the music room, I heard Mr. Decko playing the piano. I told the children they should surprise him and quietly sneak in and sit in their seats. They went in without a sound and I dashed off to the office.

A half an hour later, I went back to pick up my kids. As I approached, I heard loud voices and laughter coming from Mr. Decko's room. My children hadn't been that noisy all week, so I rushed in to see if he was having trouble.

Surprise! There was no Mr. Decko. . . just my 26 children running around, talking and playing with each other. At the piano was an old piano tuner who was blind. He must have thought all hell had broken loose when my kids arrived–but he just kept working.

I'd brought the children to their music class using the previous year's schedule. I'd totally forgotten the room was supposed to be empty at that time. I couldn't apologize enough!

Zipper Trouble

Gino was a sweet guy who loved to eat. As the kindergarten year went by, he kept getting heavier and rounder. His parents tried to keep up with his expanding waistline. They finally started buying adult-sized slacks for Gino and cutting the pant legs off because he was so short.

One day Gino came out of the bathroom with his slacks wide open. He came to my desk and said, "Mrs. Tryloff, I can't zip up my pants!"

I tried to help him. "Hold your breath," I said while I tugged at the zipper, but I couldn't get them zipped.

After struggling for five minutes, I asked, "How did your mother zip your pants this morning?"

"She laid me on the bed and told me to suck in my stomach," Gino answered.

So that's how we did it. Gino laid on his back on one of our kindergarten tables and I finally zipped up his slacks. I was in the middle of this procedure when our school secretary walked in with a note. She saw us and started to giggle. I just sighed. It was one of those "Don't ask" moments.

Chapter 5

Caught You!

Praying

As I passed out science tests, I heard Brandon mutter to himself, "God, this is going to be tough."

I gave him the evil eye and he quickly recovered. "Just praying, Mrs. Tryloff. Just praying."

Wrong House, Wrong District

Our school district bordered a large city. Many of those families wanted their children to attend our school because they thought we could provide a better education. They often gave fake addresses and sometimes their children spent a whole year with us before we'd find out they weren't paying our school taxes.

Poor Bill! He wasn't too sharp. One day he came to me very excited because his mother had painted and fixed up a new bedroom for him in the basement. I said, "That's wonderful Bill. I know you must love it. But I thought you lived in a trailer. How can your trailer have a basement?"

"Whoops! I really live in a house in the city, Mrs. Tryloff!"

I felt so sorry for the children whose parents forced them to lie to stay in our school.

Check That Check

Then there was Jane. I liked Jane so much, but I suspected she wasn't living in our school district. She was often late for school. She said her mother had to drive her to school, but according to her address on record, she was within easy walking distance.

Her mother made a real effort to fit in and help out at Jane's new school. She attended the PEP Club meetings and volunteered for our annual Christmas bazaar. There was a sweatshirt at the bazaar that she wanted to buy for herself but she didn't have enough cash. She wrote out a check to the PEP Club to pay for it. Bingo! On the check was Jane's real address. The next semester, Jane was attending her old school again.

Ambush Andy

One early spring day, I noticed some of the boys coming out of the bathroom with their pants wet across the knees. They never said anything about it, and I couldn't figure out what had happened.

Then one afternoon, little William, one of my smallest boys, came up to me screaming, "Andy peed in my face!"

I got Andy out of the bathroom and demanded to know if it was true. Andy just said, "I slipped and missed the toilet."

I told him he'd better not slip again.

The next day my boys stayed dry, but a few guys from another class were wet. We finally discovered my Andy was "Ambush Andy." He went into the bathroom by himself and quietly waited for the next customer to walk in. He would then ambush him and spray his pants across the knees. He thought it was great fun and was really getting good at it. The guys were so impressed with Andy's amazing talent they never reported him even though their pants were sprayed.

The only reason Andy was discovered was because William was so short and Andy aimed too high.

We put a stop to Andy's antics immediately.

Smoke Signals

On a cold day at recess, I saw Aaron walking around with his hand to his mouth pretending to smoke a cigarette. I walked over to him and asked what he was doing.

"Smoking. Can't you see the smoke?"

He was puffing into the frigid air making a small cloud.

I told him, "Please promise me you'll never smoke. You know it's not good for your health."

He thought a moment and said, "Okay, now I'm an Indian and these are my smoke signals."

Long Breakfast ☺

Our school had a free breakfast program in the morning for any needy children. One morning, Sharon was acting up. She screamed, kicked, and hung on to her mother. She just didn't want to come to school that day. Her mother was beside herself because she was going to be late for work.

Finally, she said, "Sharon has given me such a hard time this morning. She wouldn't get out of bed, brush her teeth, or get dressed for school. Please let her eat breakfast and then give her a time out before she goes to the playground."

Sharon sullenly sat down and ate her bowl of cereal. Then she asked for another, and another. By her fifth bowl, one of the high school helpers caught on. Since Sharon didn't want to sit alone in the corner for ten minutes while the other children played, she was cleverly delaying her time out. She decided she'd just keep eating until the bell rang for school to start.

Lost and Found Mittens ☺

One freezing winter day, William had no mittens to wear. I felt so sorry for him I grabbed a pair from our Lost and Found box and asked him to wear them home until he could find his own. He refused at first, but hated to put up a fuss in front of the class so he finally put them on.

The next morning, I received a nice note from his mother thanking me for finding William's mittens. She said he'd lost them two weeks ago. He hadn't realized they were his when I pulled them out of the Lost and Found box.

Lipstick

Usually in the spring, I'd have two or three third-grade girls appear wearing lipstick. They probably borrowed it from their older sisters or mothers and put it on after they'd left the house.

I'd go to their desk as soon as the whole class was quietly at work and whisper to the girl, "Third graders aren't allowed to wear lipstick. I won't tell your mother if you wash it off on your bathroom break. Maybe your mother will let you wear lipstick in fifth of sixth grade."

That little speech worked like a charm! I would never see bright lips on those girls again. I can't believe that not one girl ever challenged me or told her mother what happened. I think their mothers were glad I helped keep their young girls sweet and natural a little while longer.

God Bless America

It was Monday morning and we were standing beside our chairs starting to recite the Pledge of Allegiance when I noticed Janice bless herself first. Sheepishly, she looked around to see if anyone else noticed. I had to smile because I knew her family were good Catholics.

Another morning, Robert was saying the Pledge with us and when we were finished, he automatically added, "Amen."

After all, our government does need all the prayers it can get.

Chapter 6

Field Trips

Emergency Lunches

When we were going on an all-day field trip or just to the park for our last day of school picnic, I would always have a few children who would forget their lunches. Sometimes if the children received free lunches, there was nothing at home to bring for a lunch. I would pack a bag with a loaf of bread, jars of peanut butter and jelly and a few plastic knives.

As soon as someone noticed everyone was carrying a sack lunch except him, he'd panic. I'd say, "Don't worry. I've got something special for you."

On an empty desk in the back of the room, I'd set up the sandwich ingredients and some plastic wrap. I'd say, "Make a sandwich just the way you like it."

Their faces would light up. I'd often have a few kids from other classes come in to make a sandwich, too.

When we finally were eating our lunches, the child with the peanut butter sandwich was really popular. Most of his friends would feel sorry for him and offer him some of their chips, fruit, candy, and cookies. He'd always end up with more food than anyone else. I even saw a girl trade her peanut butter and jelly sandwich for a delicious-looking ham and cheese sandwich. The ham and cheese owner said, "My mother always makes me eat a nutritious sandwich. I never get peanut butter and jelly!"

Embarrassing Parents

One of my favorite field trips was to the Big Boy restaurant headquarters which was close enough for us to walk there. Many of the parents and relatives of my children worked there.

We were walking through the food preparation rooms and came to the shrimp cleaning area. Marie's mother was working in the room behind a large glass wall. When she saw Marie, she came close to the glass and smiled. To get Marie's attention, she started waving a limp shrimp at her. Some children noticed her and said, "Marie, isn't that your mom?"

Marie was embarrassed and her face turned red, but she said, "Yes."

Her mother got so excited that she took another shrimp in her other hand and waved both shrimps at us. As we all waved back, she called over her coworkers and they started waving shrimp at us, too. Marie just turned a deeper shade of red and wanted to die!

Jam Session

On the same Big Boy field trip, we walked into a refrigerated room where they were making hamburger patties. The men working in this area were recent immigrants. Some of them had beards and were dressed strangely. Half of them couldn't speak English.

The children were fascinated by the round meat balls rolling down the conveyor belt and being smashed into patties by a huge machine. As they were smashed, the machine made a sound like a clap in steady rhythm. After about two minutes of watching, one of my more active boys picked up the rhythm and started clapping. Soon the whole class was clapping and moving like a rap group. The workers were thrilled and grinned from ear to ear and started clapping in time and dancing, too. Some even picked up spoons and clanked them against pipes. We all had a real jam session. No generation or cultural gap that day!

My Husband?

Our third-grade social studies class wrote letters to a class in Ohio. We walked to our post office to mail them and toured the back area where mail is sorted. As we were leaving, my Uncle Herb walked in and was delighted to see me and have a chance to meet my class. We talked for a minute and he gave me a quick kiss as he left.

The children were strangely quiet and observant. As soon as we left, they started asking me questions about my husband. I kept telling them he was my Uncle Herb. I couldn't convince them otherwise. They kept insisting he was my husband because "he kissed you."

The rest of the year, whenever I talked about my husband, Jerry, they still thought my Uncle Herb was my husband. They would say, "We know him. He works at our post office."

We All Fall Down

Every year, our PEP Club would rent a roller skating rink for the students and their families to use after school.

Joshua and his older brother were wild on wheels and schemed to have some fun. They'd pretend to fall down and sprawled across all lanes causing a major pile-up of skaters colliding when they couldn't stop in time.

I could've wrung their necks! I pulled them off the floor and explained how dangerous their antics were and could cause broken bones or chipped teeth.

Of course, they had all kinds of excuses: "We didn't mean to fall." "We were just learning to skate." "Joshua tripped me." "I fell over a kindergartener." And "Everyone was skating too slowly."

As I skated past Betsy who was sitting on the floor after taking a spill, she told me, "My feet took off without my body."

Career Hero

Steven was a popular, lively boy liked by everyone. His father and mother looked and lived like hippies. They had long hair, ate natural foods and got around on bicycles. I'm not even sure if they were married because the mother had a different last name and Steven's father called her "my lady."

Steven's father worked for the city and drove a garbage truck. Every toy Steven brought in for sharing was said to have come from a garbage can on his father's route. If I mentioned I liked his shirt, he'd tell me, "Isn't it great! Someone threw it away and Dad found it for me." His father was definitely a hero in Steven's eyes.

One day, Steven asked me if his father could bring in the city garbage truck for Show and Tell. "Sounds great!" I said.

The next Friday, Steven's father parked the truck right outside our room. He was so proud of his job. First, he gave a short speech and then entertained questions. Kindergarteners get right down to basics when asking questions:

"Did you ever find a body in a garbage can?"

"How much money do you make?" (By the way–more than I was making!)

"Doesn't it stink?"

Mr. Addison answered every question seriously and honestly. He allowed the kids to sit in the seats and pull the levers to compact the garbage. The kids loved the noise, smells, and hands-on experience. It was the children's most popular field trip. After that day, everyone wanted to drive a garbage truck when they grew up!

JOANN TRYLOFF

Bring Money

Every year, we searched for some new, different, and free field trips for the children. We tried to take three trips a year and usually had money to go on only one paid trip. Just before Easter, we decided to visit a local candy maker that had been in the area forever and looked interesting. Usually, we didn't allow the kids to bring any money with them so no one would feel left out when someone bought candy or a toy. We should've realized we were in trouble when the candy company sent permission slips to be signed by the parents and it kept mentioning that the children would be allowed to shop in their store after the tour. We finally gave in and permitted the children to bring some money.

The day of the field trip arrived and so did the money! Some of the children had twenty dollars in their hands, but about six had no money at all. Ninety-eight third graders had dollar bills and change stuffed in pockets, mittens, wallets, purses, and tied up in hankies. Children were counting it, playing with it, and losing it. Dimes rolled across the desks and onto the floor. The children didn't pay attention to their lessons because they were busy recounting their money to be sure it was still all there. Some of the children were accused of stealing another's money. "But I just found it on the floor," they would cry.

We finally got the kids on the bus and into the candy factory. The tour was short and sweet. We walked along a hallway with windows on one side which allowed us to see the people making certain Easter candies. Above each window was a plaque telling what process was being performed. The whole tour took about twenty minutes. Then we were funneled into a giant, brightly-lit room—the gift shop! The kids took off like jets! They were promised fifteen minutes to shop and they didn't want to waste one second!

The gift shop contained very expensive chocolates and stuffed animals, baskets and toys of all kinds. The children were picking up adorable stuffed animals and running to show their friends. When they realized how expensive the animals were, they would try to remember where to return them. I spotted several room mothers with arms full of these beautiful stuffed animals given to them by the children saying, "I can't remember where this goes."

I really loved the machines where you could slide a trap door and dump some candy into your bag. The kids loved working it but the bag always weighed more than they could afford, and we had to figure out a way to put the candy back into the bins.

In all the hustle and bustle, I noticed kind Carolyn slip her friend, Jean, two quarters to buy something. Jean had forgotten her money. I also saw many children sharing their treats with those who couldn't buy any.

The check-out lines were long and soon it was well past the time we were supposed to leave. The bus drivers were having a fit because we weren't on the bus. The fifteen-minute shopping time had stretched to thirty minutes. Even then, a few children were complaining they didn't have enough time to spend all of their money.

Finally back on the bus and it was trading and tasting time. Some generous children would share their candy with those who did not buy any. Even though I suggested they save some candy to put in their family's Easter baskets, it was disappearing fast. The kids had a wonderful time and said it was the greatest field trip they ever took.

Chapter 7

Fads—They Come and Go

Clothing Fads

As a teacher for many years, I've seen it all in clothes fads. When I started teaching, all the girls wore dresses or pleated skirts, blouses, and sweaters. They wore anklets and sturdy shoes which their mothers polished for them. Tights weren't invented yet and nylons weren't worn until seventh or eighth grades, and even then, just for special occasions. The boys wore corduroy pants, slacks, shirts, and sweaters. Everyone would have to change out of their school clothes when they got home before they could go out to play.

Gradually, casualness crept in. I bless the day teachers were allowed to wear pantsuits to school. Not sweaters or blouses and slacks. We had to have a jacket or something that covered our bottoms. Pantsuits were so comfortable compared to the short dresses and skirts we were wearing during the 1960s. We could even sneak on a pair of knee-high nylons and not have to be totally encased in pantyhose for the day.

I was happy to see the girls wearing slacks because they were now free to participate in sports activities and get more exercise.

Designer jeans soon arrived. They cost three or four times as much as regular K-Mart or Sears jeans. The more fashion-conscious kids had to have them. Once they had a pair, they'd wear them every day, flaunting the designer's name in the face of the others. Kindergarteners! I'm talking four and five-year-olds who already knew how to be snobbish. I always went out of my way to comment on any child's jeans which didn't bear a designer label.

Pretty, long-haired Linda stood in front of the group for sharing time. She told the class she had new jeans on, and then turned around to show off the label on the jean's pocket. I said she was sure lucky her mother was so nice to get her some new clothes. Linda was exasperated that I didn't notice they were Jordache jeans. She said, "But Mrs. Tryloff, look!"

Then she stuck her little bottom in my face so I couldn't miss the label.

Clothes fads got worse as the years rolled on. I remember jeans so torn and ripped that you could see skin or underwear beneath them. Then there were the t-shirts the children wore with their jeans. Once in a while, they'd wear a t-shirt with a gross word on it or an obscene gesture. I'd either have them turn the shirt inside out or they'd have to wear one of our old paint shirts over it. I don't know what their parents were thinking when they let their children out of the house with those shirts on, or if they even knew what their children were wearing to school.

I'll never forget that first pair of sneakers that lit up when the kids walked. My children were getting lined up for music class and I kept seeing flashes. I really thought my eyes were going crazy. Within a month, my kindergarten line flashed like a conga line of lightning bugs as we walked down the halls.

Great Inventions

Velcro was one of the greatest inventions of all time! The children could dress themselves more easily. Although there were days when the kindergarten class sat on the floor while I read a story and half of them would play with the Velcro strips on their sneakers. At times it got so noisy, I had to ask them to please stop so I wouldn't get hoarse.

I remember sewing strips of Velcro in a hand-me-down coat one recess as I watched the children play outside. For one month, poor Jade had worn this coat in freezing weather with a broken zipper. Every time I saw that coat flapping wide open, I'd ask her to have her parents fix it or get another coat for her. I knew her family didn't have much money, so one day, I just took care of it myself.

Another great idea was putting plastic bags over the children's shoes so they could slide into boots that were too small or wet. I'd always keep extra plastic bags on hand just in case. Teachers become very creative when faced with problems that take time out of the teaching day.

Black Jack Gum

During one school year, I started a Black Jack gum fad.

I had a prize bag containing packages of gum, Lifesavers, and candy bars. I'd let the kids choose one of these prizes if they got their work completed for the week. One of the treats was old-fashioned Black Jack gum. My neighbor had some free samples from work and gave them to me for my prize bag. The gum was black colored and licorice flavored. The children never heard of it and didn't like it. I noticed my prize bag was getting low and not much was left except the Black Jack gum.

I had an idea! At lunch one day, I chewed a stick of Black Jack and when the children came in, I smiled at them. Most of the kids noticed I'd lost one of my front teeth. They were all upset until I said, "Fooled you!" I told them when I was in third grade, I'd chew a stick of Black Jack gum and work it with my tongue to cover one of my front teeth and surprise my friends. I said I especially like it at Halloween time when I was a witch, a bum, or a scarecrow.

That Friday at reward time, the Black Jack gum was a prized possession!

The Gloved Wonder

Remember when the boy wonder Michael Jackson sang and pranced on stage flashing his one glove? The older kids started to appear on the playground wearing glittery gloves. It wasn't too long until my younger children wanted to be "cool" too. Sure enough, they showed up with a glove they'd borrowed from their brothers or talked their mothers into buying for them. Some just wore one winter glove to school.

They wanted to wear their gloves constantly and tried to sneak them on in the classroom. As the weeks went by, these gloves got stained and dirty. The children would wear their one glove during class time, trying to write with it on, eat with it on, and I once caught George pasting his project together while wearing his Michael Jackson glove.

My patience was starting to wear thin! During the third week of this silliness, the boys started to leave their gloves at home. Thank heavens. I know their parents, gym teachers, and cafeteria ladies were as happy as I was when the single glove craze had finally ended.

Chapter 8

Holidays

Keeping a Secret

Secrets and holidays go together. But keeping a secret is almost impossible for a child. I'd always help the children make Christmas and Mother's Day gifts which we'd wrap before they took them home. I'd lay all the ground work to make the gift a surprise. I'd explain that the gift was a special secret and we wouldn't tell our parents about it so they'd be surprised when they unwrapped it on Christmas morning. I'd instruct the children to hide the gift in a drawer in their bedroom until it was time to give it to their parents. Even if their mother saw it while she was putting clothes away, she wouldn't know what it was because it was all wrapped up.

I think half of the children carried their gifts home and made their parents open them right away. They were so excited! Mothers would walk their children to school and stop in and thank me for the super gift the very next day. I'd sigh and say, "Mother's Day isn't until Sunday. Paul wasn't supposed to give it to you until then."

Some mothers admitted they couldn't wait to open their beautifully wrapped gifts.

One mother said Jan ran home the day we started the gift project and blurted out, "Mrs. Tryloff told us a secret. We're making Mother's Day books and we're not to tell a soul."

Easter Surprises

Once in a while, I was lucky enough to be able to kid around and trade jokes with my class. They took time to enjoy a good laugh but didn't lose control and bounce off the walls the rest of the day.

One particular year, my group was a fun-loving, clever bunch. It was our turn to decorate the glass showcase for Easter, so we decided to make paper flowers and decorate eggs to lay in the green Easter grass. Some of the children brought in their stuffed rabbits and an Easter basket. The showcase looked great, and as I closed the sliding glass door, I told them I was proud of how well they worked to create such a lovely showcase.

The next day, as I walked to class to gym, Tyler said, "Mrs. Tryloff, look what those rabbits did in our showcase."

I noticed his friends were holding back giggles and Tyler's eyes were sparkling. Sometime earlier, he must have sprinkled a package of chocolate-covered raisins around the rabbits. The class and I howled!

The following day, my clever girls started getting into the act. They brought in some small stuffed bunnies and placed them by the larger rabbits. When the class noticed the extra bunnies, Emily informed us, "I guess that's what happens when you leave rabbits alone all night. My mother says rabbits have lots of babies."

Word got around school quickly and kids and teachers from other classrooms would casually drift by to check on the changing scene in our popular Easter showcase.

Dead Eggs

When the afternoon class came in, I was all set up to help them dye Easter eggs. I had four cups of different colors on each table and told the children, "This is how we dye the eggs. Very carefully put your egg in the cup that has the color you want. Then come over here in the reading corner and I'll read *Peter Cottontail* to you while the color gets nice and dark. When the story is over, we can go to our cups and check on our eggs."

As soon as the story was finished, the children anxiously ran to their tables and lifted up their eggs. Julie just looked at hers and wouldn't touch it. When I asked her why, she replied, "I know you said we were going to dye them, but I'm not sure if mine is dead yet."

All That Halloween Candy

For a youngster in grade school, Halloween is second only to Christmas. They love wearing a costume and acting wild and crazy. Plus they get to go begging for all that great candy crackling in the bottom of their pillowcase. They've earned the right to all their loot, fair and square, by yelling, "Trick OR Treat!" hidden behind a mask while shivering under a flimsy costume.

These are the expert opinions from my second grade on the good, the bad, and the ugly candy:

Awesome–M&M's, Tootsie Pops, Snickers, Three Musketeers, and Hershey's Cookies and Cream.

Jessica was surprised and happy with money. "I usually get it from old people," she said.

Brian scoffed, "They probably just ran out of candy."

Samantha was thrilled with a metallic pencil, but Andrew interrupted, "No way! To be good it's got to have sugar. A lot of sugar. Not something you can use in school."

Just Okay–Only good for trading or letting your parents munch on: Reese's peanut butter cups, potato chips (no sugar), Starburst, Twizzlers, gum, Skittles, Pixie Sticks.

Totally Gross–Untouchables. Won't even give it to the dog! Yogurt-covered raisins, apples (way too healthy), Mounds and Almond Joy bars (yuck–coconut), Good'n'Plenty "Anything licorice is disgusting and stinky. Did you ever smell it? It tastes even worse!"

Hannah was fussy about texture. "I hate anything that melts or anything squishy or if it's too creamy or caramelly."

After rating their candy, the children told me their special hiding places where no one could touch their hoard, let alone munch on it.

Vern hid his in a little cupboard in their computer room. He said, "It's not so much my little sister I'm worried about. My mother's the one. She's got a real sweet tooth. I took all my M&M's and put them in a sock."

Matthew didn't trust anyone. "I take my pillowcase to bed and pretend to fall asleep on it and then I can munch all night if I want to. Don't tell my mom!" he implored.

Megan wasn't allowed to have any candy in her room. "My family is pretty honest," she told the class. "I put my name on the bag and then write 'Do Not Touch'–just in case."

How long did their sweet treasures last? Karla said once she hoarded the last bit of candy until summer. John said, "I throw away the crummy stuff just before Easter. You always get a new supply then."

Zachary bragged, "Mine only lasted one day because I ate it all. But then I got really sick."

Everyone groaned in compassion.

The Magic Broom

My friend, Jean, who taught the other kindergarten class, was always ready for a practical joke. She had a great sense of humor. Jean would try anything once. I often got carried away and went along with her ideas.

One morning a couple of weeks before Halloween, she walked in with this scraggly broom that she'd bought for 29 cents. "Doesn't this look like a witch's broom?" she asked. "Why don't you get dressed up like a witch for our Halloween party and come into my room looking for your broom? The kids will go wild!"

"I think not," I said.

Little did I know the commotion that broom would cause in the years to come. Jean would stand the broom in a corner of her room.

When the children would ask about it, she'd say she didn't know where it came from. It just appeared. Since it was near Halloween, one of the brighter kids would think it might be a witch's broom because they always made witches riding on brooms out of construction paper.

Jean noticed the children would always keep their eyes on the broom when they were near that corner and stay their distance. No one dared touch it.

Rumors started spreading. My children were talking about the magic broom in Mrs. Trent's room that gave off a spark. They were convinced the broom was magic and surely belonged to a witch.

One day, we were in Jean's room singing and the children couldn't keep their minds on the song. They kept staring at that broom! Another day, we wrote a story together about where the broom came from and to whom it belonged. The day after Halloween, the broom was gone, never to be seen again that school year. That confirmed the rumor. Some witch took it for a ride on Halloween night!

Year after year, the broom appeared about two weeks before Halloween. Sometimes, it would be in my room for a few days. The children would always close the closet doors between the two kindergarten rooms to make sure the broom wouldn't travel during the night. They'd come in the next morning and check all around the room to see if it was hidden in any of the corners.

One day the broom was resting high on top of a cupboard near the door to the playground. Most of the children were outside for recess but I'd kept three kids inside to help them with their lessons. I was sitting in the doorway so I could watch the others. All of a sudden, a gust of wind came in and blew the broom down. It bounced on the floor, just missing me.

The three children screamed and jumped to run out of the room. Of course, I didn't touch the broom. I just let it lie there because I had told the children I really didn't know what would happen if someone touched it. By the next day, the rumor all over school was that the broom had gotten mad and hit a teacher.

Jean and I were in stitches! We even had parents and administrators ask about the broom. We would just smile, shrug our shoulders, and offer no explanations. We stuck to the story that the broom showed up around Halloween and disappeared the day after.

After about ten years of this fun, Jean retired and I moved to third grade. I inherited the broom and I continued its tradition with the third graders. There are hundreds of creative writing stories out there about its origin and powers. Yes, about four brave third graders have actually bragged that they touched the broom—either on a dare or when no one was looking. Brian bragged he got a bad shock from it.

When high schoolers came back to visit me at Open House, they'd get a sheepish look on their face and waited until no one was near before they'd ask if the broom still appeared. I know some were still convinced that the witch's broom was full of magic. The myth lives on.

Letters to Santa ☺

As the children got older, I'd find more and more of them were suspicious about Santa. But they always protected themselves, just in case.

In early December, we would write letters to Santa. The children loved writing them and I always loved to read them and would share the cutest ones with other teachers, my husband, and my friends. Here are some of my favorite "Letters to Santa":

- ❄ I know you have many new names on your list, so if you need help finding me, I'm sure you can ask Grandpa. You see, he's had sixty-five Christmases and I'm sure he knows the rules.
- ❄ A chatty letter from Rocky: Santa, you know what I want for Christmas is a super, duper, double looper. That's all I want. How are the elves? Tell them to make me that, okay? If you are real, thanks for all the presents you gave me. P. S. Write me sometime. See you at the mall. Rocky

- This one from a worrier: Santa, please don't drink and drive on Christmas Eve. I hope you don't get hurt while you are riding in your sleigh. Please wear your seatbelt and brush your teeth.
- Dear Santa, For Christmas I would like Cathy Cut and Curl salon. Also Baby Barbie slurp. Space Ranger puppet. Buzz Lightyear. I'll tell you the rest when I see you. Jessica
- Nicholas had such good manners. He didn't ask for anything for himself, just his mother and baby sister: Santa, Mommy wants a new house so I do, too. My sister Amanda wants a new dollhouse because she's going to be a girl when she gets bigger. How's Rudolph? And all your reindeers? Is Mrs. Claus okay? Thanks for the toys I got last year. Nicholas
- Jerry buttered Santa up with a poem: Santa, I think I was good this year. Here's a little poem for you.

Roses are red, violets are blue
I'm sure lucky to have a best friend like you

Then followed "the list". . .

- Brett wanted it all: Dear Santa, I want a Sega Genesis, and I want all the wrestlers, and I want you to make all the homeless get food, clothing and money and shelter and rich. And I want a wish. I want to be a hockey player and a baseball player and I want my soccer team to come in first place. That's all. Love, your friend, Brett
- Third grader Patrick tried to sneak in a request for a girlfriend: Dear Santa, I want the Batman Returns movie, x-ray glasses, a girlfriend, Ren and Stimpy toys, and a hockey stick. Thanks, Patrick

Gifts

Gifts! Crazy, wonderful, sweet, silly, cheap, expensive, ugly, delicate, handmade, beautiful, surprising, lopsided, broken, used, chipped, funny, weird, smelly, and even useful gifts! Teachers receive all kinds of gifts, especially at Christmas. Every year I was thrilled to open the surprises they and their parents had picked out for me. The kids and I made a big deal out of shaking and feeling and trying to guess what was in each package before I opened it. The giver was so excited and giggling like crazy while we guessed wild things. Sometimes they'd turn out to be quite a surprise. One gift was guessed to be bubble bath but was actually a great bottle of wine. I've received boxes of chocolates with bites taken out of some of the pieces, a Superman watch which I really loved and wore a lot, a pretty sexy see-through negligee, and lots and lots of jewelry.

The last day before Christmas vacation I often had six pins on my sweater, two extra bracelets on my arm, three new necklaces, and too many earrings to wear. I looked like a walking Christmas tree! One year I got yellow fuzzy duck slippers that quacked when I walked. I wore them all day long. Very warm and comfy, but noisy.

The True Spirit of Christmas ☺

One particular year, the preschool teacher told our staff that all the children in her program were truly needy. Most of the children would not even have a decent Christmas dinner, let alone any gifts from Santa. Our school decided to adopt the preschool class and make sure Christmas would be special for them.

From October to December, we had bake sales, raffles, a donkey basketball game with the staff, and Santa's Special Shop. All the profits were used to buy gifts for the class. We had a drawing to see which class would shop for the children's gifts, which class would wrap the gifts, and which would invite the preschoolers to their class party and pass out the gifts.

Our class was the lucky one chosen to give out the gifts. What fun! We had collected enough money to give each child several gifts of toys, clothing, and other surprises. After all the excitement, I allowed my children to play with the younger ones and their new toys until the school day was over.

We all noticed a small, four-year-old boy quietly scurrying around trading his presents with his classmates. We couldn't figure out why Josh didn't like his gifts. Everything was chosen especially for him. His mother had given us his letter to Santa. When I noticed he traded his biggest gift, a dump truck, to Sarah for her doll, I was really bewildered.

George, being one of my bolder boys, went up to Josh and asked, "Why don't you like your new toys?"

Josh shyly answered, "I don't need all these toys. I'm keeping the teddy bear and Candyland, but I'm trading the rest to get something nice for my brothers and sisters at home. Mom and I can wrap everything and surprise them on Christmas Day."

What an angel!

By the next day, my entire class knew about Josh's gift trading. They had glimpsed the true spirit of Christmas.

Chapter 9

Play on Words

Eternity Leave

Sharon came to school one morning as happy as could be. She told me her mother, who was working at the post office, was going to be home all the time. "She's taking eternity leave. Now she's going to be home when the new baby gets here."

Stolen Song ☺

The kindergarten children were all sitting around on the floor as we started learning our ABCs in order.
I started to sing the ABC Song. As I got to the letter "P," I stopped and asked them to sing that much with me. Most already knew the tune and joined right in.
Molly raised her hand and said, "That's Twinkle, Twinkle Little Star."
Dan waved his hand at me and blurted out, "Did you steal the Twinkle song?"

Fractions are Easy ☺

8 = ******** was on the board.
"What do you think half of eight would be?" I asked.
Johnny raised his hand and eagerly answered, "It's a circle."
"What do you mean?"
"Maybe it's a zero?"
"Come here and show me," I asked him.
"See!" Johnny exclaimed as he put his hand over the bottom portion of the 8.

Shapes ☺

Teaching kindergarteners shapes was always fun. I'd often hear "box" for a square, and "round" or "wheel" for a circle. Rectangles were called a "long box" or a "house." Triangle was a killer to remember. "Tepee" or "tent" was always a good guess. David knew it started with "tri" so he came up with "tricycle." It was the only "tri" word he knew.

Counting Catastrophes ☺

I was testing my kindergarteners to see if they could count all the way to twenty-five in order to receive their special star badge. Kathy was doing great and made it through the teens, which was difficult. Then she finished with, "Twenty, twenty-one, twenty-tooth, twenty-three, twenty-four, twenty-five."
She proudly grinned at me. "Wasn't that perfect, Mrs. Tryloff?"
Then there was Gina trying to count to fifty for a special award. "Twenty-eight, twenty-nine, twenty-ten."
When I asked Shawn to count to twenty-five for his star badge, he confidently said, "No problem Mrs. Tryloff. My Grandma taught me my numbers years ago. 1, 2, 3, 4, 5, 6, 7, 8, 9, 10, Jack, Queen, King." Oh no!

All of a sudden, he realized what he was saying and we both broke out laughing.

"I'll bet your Grandma is a good card player, too," I told him.

Cricket in my Neck ☺

We were taking our yearly kindergarten test that was given in 45-minute sections. It was tough for the kids to sit and concentrate that long. Toward the end of the first section, I saw Christopher rub the back of his neck and say to Duane, "I have a cricket in my neck."

Three-Oh ☺

As we were singing our favorite Christmas songs, April raised her hand and said, "I can sing Jingle Bells all by myself."

She stood up and sang her song and I told the children, "When you sing all by yourself, we call that a solo."

Katie piped up and said, "I can sing it too."

I told her to join April and they could sing together. I said, "When two people sing a song together we call it a duo. Does anyone know what you call three people singing together?"

Denny waved his hand, "I know! It's a three-oh!"

Abracadabra ☺

We had a moment before leaving for home and I was going over all the "magic words." As we reviewed them, I heard: "please," "thank you," "excuse me," and "I'm sorry." There was a lull as everyone was trying to think of more and then Tom yelled out, "I know another–Abracadabra!"

Fish Feet ☺

During kindergarten sharing time, Dan told the class he went fishing in Florida with his dad and they caught an eight-foot fish.

Roger blurted out, "No way! Fish don't have feet!"

Puppet ☺

We were going through the names of animals and what we call their babies.

"Cat–kitten"
"Duck–duckling"
"Horse–pony"
"Dog–puppy"

Cindy raised her hand and said, "A really new puppy is called a puppet."

Mowing Slows Him Down ☺

The kindergarten class was going over all the things they had to do to get ready for school in the morning.

Vince raised his hand and told us, "I can always get ready before my dad because I don't have to mow my face like he does."

With Love ☺

The children were playing a game where they picked up an alphabet block and had to tell the class words that began with their letters.

When it was Doug's turn, he grabbed an "O" and an "X" and quickly piped up with "hugs" and "kisses." The class accepted his words and the game continued without a break.

MY HEART BELONGS TO TEACHING

Pliers Please ☺

I was sitting on a swing as the kindergarteners played during recess. Donny came running up to me holding out his thumb.
"Mrs. Tryloff, I have a splinter in my thumb. Can you get some pliers and take it out?"

Honey Pudding ☺

I was reading *The Three Bears* to the class and I heard Jason whisper to Pat, "What's this porridge?"
Pat shrugged, "Must be a bear word for honey."

Different Country ☺

Our class was looking at a map of the United States and talking about how big our country was. The children were finding different states they had heard about and locating countries that bordered America.
A week later, Pam's mother told me their family traveled to Indiana over the weekend to visit some of Pam's relatives whom she had never met. After hours on the road, they finally arrived and were eating supper with all the cousins, aunts, and uncles.
Pam piped up and told her cousin, "Boy, it sure was a long way from my country to your country."

Brownies ☺

The children were lining up to go home. I knew a group of five girls were headed to their Brownie meeting held after school in our music room. Mona had just moved to Michigan from Nevada and had been in our class for just a week. I thought she might like to join the Brownie troop to help meet new friends. I asked Mona, "Did they have Brownies in Nevada?"

"Sure," she replied. "My Mom and I baked them all the time."

Keep Your Noses Clean ☺

Our principal asked if he could borrow three of my best guys to help set up the gym for a program. I walked down to the office area with them, and as I left, my parting words were, "Have fun. Keep your noses clean."

I turned around to wave good-bye and started laughing. John was getting a tissue out of his pocket, Bill was rubbing his nose, and Eric was starting to pick his nose.

I quickly said, "'Keep your noses clean' means be on your best behavior. Now go and do a good job."

Disargument ☺

After lunch, Steve and Cory came in red-faced and disheveled. The other kids told me they had been fighting outside. I gave them a stern look, but before I could say anything, Steve said, "It wasn't nothin', Mrs. Tryloff. We were just having a disargument."

Potty Training ☺

It was Robert's week to water the plants on the window ledge. He was anxious to help out and wanted to please me. All of a sudden, he rushed to my desk and pointed to the puddles on the window sills.

"Mrs. Tryloff, those plants aren't potty-trained yet."

Name Change ☺

The children were drawing names for our Christmas gift exchange. I had just started to explain, "Today we are exchanging names so we can. . ."

Janice had just drawn Sophie's name and interrupted me. "Mrs. Tryloff, I don't want to be called 'Sophie' and I don't want to give my name away, either."

Chapter 10

Picture Day

Picture Perfect

Every fall, we got our pictures taken for a school composite. Parents could also purchase extra pictures which made great Christmas gifts.

Picture day was always a wild experience! The children came to school all spiffed up with stiff, new, clean clothes and moussed, gelled and sprayed hair. I always commented on how great they looked. I'd say they were beautiful and so handsome. All nice and clean with shiny brushed teeth so they could light up the camera with their smiles. Honest Eric said, "We were in such a rush I didn't have time to brush my teeth, but my mother sprayed something on my front teeth and rubbed them to get the chocolate milk off."

Paul would show me how his mother rolled the sleeves of his shirt under so it would look like it fit. Jill would tell me she was wearing her older sister's skirt and showed me how her mother pinned the waist together so it would fit. Sam would say, "Mom bought me this sweater for Christmas but she gave it to me to wear for the picture. She's going to hide it again until December 25th."

Some girls would show me a necklace or a pair of earrings their mother let them borrow for the day.

The children really were keyed up as they waited to be called to have their pictures taken. It was almost impossible to teach. Some children would always forget it was picture day and wanted to go home to change clothes. Others would have forgotten their picture money and wanted to go to the office to call home and have someone bring it to them. Still others would say they were supposed to get pictures but they thought their brother or sister had their money. At least six mothers would be knocking at my door during the day to bring more money, change their order, put an extra bow in Janet's hair, or just check to see that Charles didn't get dirty during lunch time.

Some children wouldn't play the games in the gym, sit on the floor for sharing and story time, or paste and paint. They might get messed up! If their picture wasn't taken by lunch time, they all wanted to stay in because the wind might blow a strand of hair out of place during recess.

The funniest thing was that the photographer gave each child a comb while they waited in line for their picture. These children, who hadn't moved their heads all day, would start to drag that comb through their stiff hair and completely ruin their hair style. They'd comb each other's hair, change their parts, pull bows out, and loosen slicked-back cowlicks.

I was always so happy when picture day was over! The next day it was back to normal, comfortable clothes again.

Red Shoes

Kathy carried her new red shoes in her backpack and showed them to me as soon as she came in the room. I asked her to please put them on.

She said, "No! They might get dirty when I play in them. I can only wear them with my beautiful dress when I get my picture taken."

Two hours later, a fifth grader knocked on our door and told us it was picture time. The kids excitedly got in position as we lined them up according to what package they were buying, and then their height in each group. Some wanted to stand by their friends, while others argued that they were the tallest in the group. Mass confusion!

All of a sudden, Kathy burst out in tears. "I have to get my red shoes!"

I comforted her and told her, "Don't worry. The picture just shows your shoulders and head. Your shoes won't show."

"No," she bawled, "I need my new red shoes!"

I finally gave in and we all waited patiently while Kathy walked to her cubbyhole, got out her shoes, and calmly put them on. I quickly dried her tears, and at last, we all marched off to the picture room.

I hope Kathy's parents appreciated her tearless, smiling face, and those beautiful new red shoes.

Chapter 11

Simply Said

Raw Cereal ☺

    Our room mothers were treating the morning kindergarten class to a simple breakfast at the conclusion of our food and nutrition unit. They brought in boxes of cereal, milk, bananas, orange juice, and rolls. As I was going around to the tables helping the children open their milk cartons, I heard macho Bob say, "No milk for me. I like my cereal raw."

Color of the Wind ☺

    The children were coloring a spring picture to paste their kites on. Jennifer asked, "What color is the wind, Mrs. Tryloff?"

Eyebrow Tummy Ache ☺

    Nadine came to me with tears in her eyes holding her forehead. "Mrs. Tryloff. I think I've got a tummy ache in my eyebrow."

No-It-All 🙂

I returned to school after being ill for two days. The children were delighted to see me back. They all told me what a terrible substitute teacher they had to put up with.

James, our class clown, said, "Mrs. Tryloff, that substitute was a no-it-all. She said 'no' all the time."

Whoops 🙂

Heather was hastily buttoning her coat so she could be first on the playground to get her favorite swing. When she got to the top button, she looked at Janet and said, "My top button lost its hole!"

Old Stones 🙂

Our science class was looking at Stan's rock collection. The children were sorting the rocks according color and size. Stan told Tabitha, "You know, when a stone grows up, it gets to be a rock."

Cat Talk 🙂

In kindergarten, after we finished a pet unit, the children could bring their pets to school. Renee was petting her cat and saying, "Who's the puddy, puddy cat? Puddy, woody, woody kitty cat."

Joseph listened to her and asked, "Why do you talk to your cat like that?"

Renee answered, "Because cats don't understand English."

MY HEART BELONGS TO TEACHING

Change of Pace ☺

Sam said to Jerry, "Let's not tease the girls on the playground. It's boring."

Jerry replied, "Okay, today we'll just hit them."

Humming ☺

I was teaching the kindergarten class to sing "America". First I played the tune on the piano and most of the children guessed the title. Then I said, "Let's hum the tune first before we learn the words."

I would say the words and then we tried to sing them while I played piano.

The next day, we practiced "America" again. I happened to hear Dave whisper to Janet, "I like humming better than singing because you don't have to remember all those words."

Lick Quick ☺

During the last week of school, the PEP Club mothers treated our class to ice cream cones. We went out to the playground to eat them because it was so hot that day.

Brian was a sticky, drippy mess when I overheard him say to Katherine, "Big cones are fun to eat, but they are quicker than I can lick."

Family Resemblance ☺

Jill was telling me about a family reunion her family went to on Memorial Day. She was really impressed by how much her dad looked like his brother. She put it this way.

"My Uncle John looks like Daddy's face."
I understood immediately what she meant.

Recycling Revolt ☺

My class was sharing recycling ideas during science time. The children were coming up with some great ideas they'd either seen or heard–frozen orange juice cans for pencil holders, plastic grocery bags to line wastepaper baskets, newspaper for the bottom of a birdcage and rolled newspapers for the fireplace.

Barb raised her hand, "My mom's really good at recycling. Too good! I have to wear my sister's hand-me-down clothes and we have to eat leftovers for supper."

Out of Smarts ☺

Our school was giving an important test that took about two hours a day for four consecutive days. On the third day, as I walked past Erin, she was sitting there just staring off into space. I whispered, "What's the matter? Are you stuck on something?"

Erin sighed and said, "I think I just ran out of smarts."

When You Grow Up ☺

An author was visiting our school. She was talking to my children after reading a book to them. She asked Sam what he wanted to be when he grew up.

"Taller" he promptly replied.

MY HEART BELONGS TO TEACHING

Forced Enlistment

It was the first day of first grade and Matthew had cried continuously all morning. He definitely wasn't happy to be back to school.

By afternoon, he still hadn't stopped crying. I went to him and tried to console him, "It's okay. You're a grown-up first-grade boy now. You're old enough to go to school all day."

He looked at me with panic in his eyes and wailed, "All day! All year! Who signed me up for this!"

Season Ticket ☺

Walter and his music teacher must have had a real personality clash. Almost every week, Walter would leave the music room with his head hanging down and a detention slip in his hand.

One day I heard him tell his best friend, "Mr. Faye might as well give me a season ticket to noon hour detention. It would save him a lot of writing them out every week."

Chapter 12

Talent

Talent Is in the Nose of the Beholder

One day, my children came in from lunch hour all excited. They told me about this great trick that Adam could do.

"When Adam drinks his chocolate milk, he can squirt it back out his nose," Dawn told me. "It's gross but sooooo cool."

Adam remained a cafeteria hero for the rest of the year. I heard he gave many command performances.

Junior Ad Executive

The third-grade class was busy making posters to advertise our Christmas boutique. Sara, thinking like a future businesswoman, wondered out loud, "How much do you think a TV commercial would cost?"

Stand by Your Talent

I knew Patricia was taking an art class downtown on Saturdays. She definitely was talented! One day, I asked her to draw a snowman for the class and I'd put it in a special frame. I gave her a picture of some cute snowmen I'd seen in a magazine to get her started. When Patricia brought her drawing to my desk, it was nothing like the magazine picture I'd shown her. I praised her drawing and then said, "Maybe you want to add some color to this picture?"

Patricia firmly said, "No, it doesn't need color. See how I shaded it with my pencil. We've been studying shading in my art class. That's all it needs."

She was so right! I was totally off base thinking she would try to copy the "cute" picture I'd given her. That's what I would try to do because I had no talent or self-confidence. And then I asked her to color a beautifully shaded masterpiece that was uniquely hers!

I was awed by her talent and asked her to please sign and date her picture because I was going to keep it forever. I told her she was going to be famous some day and I'd be so proud to tell everyone I knew her when she was six years old.

A Real Cowboy

Each afternoon, the whole school had a fifteen-minute silent reading period when you could read anything you wanted. Near the back of the room, I noticed Dave, my budding artist, quietly drawing during his reading time.

I quietly walked near his desk and took the picture he was working on out of the book where it was hidden. It was a little risqué for school, but wonderful!

Dave had such a delightful sense of humor to go with his artistic talent. I hope his talents are still being put to good use today.

Chapter 13

Out of the Mouth of Babes

Frog in Throat ☺

    I was singing with my children when all of a sudden, I started to lose my voice. I said, "Wait just a second. I think I have a frog in my throat."
    I went to our water fountain to get a drink. Shelley whispered to Ellen, "I think she's trying to drown that frog."

Hungry Pencil Sharpener ☺

    "Jimmy, that's about the tenth time you've sharpened your pencil today," I said.
    "I know Mrs. Tryloff. That pencil sharpener is really hungry today," Jimmy replied.

How Old?

    Timmy and Jacob were whispering and giggling as they tried to guess how old their music teacher was. To them, she seemed *really* old. Finally, as the class lined up to leave the music room, they went to her desk together and Timmy said, "We'll tell you how old we are if you tell us how old you are."

Plant Some Birds ☺

In February, we started talking about the birds that stayed in Michigan during the winter. I brought in some birdseed and we made a simple birdfeeder which we put near the window. Each morning we watched to see what kinds of birds appeared.

On the third day, it was Josh's turn to run out and put the birdseed in the feeder. When he came back in, he tugged at my sleeve and seriously asked, "If we're going to grow birds, shouldn't we put the seeds in the ground?"

Peas on the Cob ☺

As I was walking out of the lunchroom with my tray, I heard Ryan say, "Ugh, peas!"

He carefully stuck them in a glob of mashed potatoes so they wouldn't contaminate the rest of the food on his plate.

William said, "Well, if they'd put peas on a cob like corn, maybe you'd like them better."

Disappearing Act ☺

The kindergarten classes were sitting on the floor watching a magician perform his tricks. He'd just made a rabbit disappear into his hat. Michael raised his hand and blurted out, "Can you make Cory disappear too? He's kicking and pinching me."

Name that Chick Quick

Our class went on a field trip to a nearby farm. We followed the farmer into a large chicken coop that held at least 200 chickens. The farmer handed Jan a baby chick to hold and she asked, "What's this chick's name?"

"Yeah. What are all these chickens' names?" Rob asked the poor farmer.

Once Upon A Time

I'd just started reading a fairy tale to my kindergarten children. Sean raised his hand and asked, "How long ago was 'once upon a time'?"

Relatively Speaking ☺

First graders Gary and James were discussing their families at recess. Gary informed James, "Did you know you can't marry a relative?"

James, who was always a quick thinker, replied, "Yes you can. My Mom and Dad are married."

Set It Free ☺

Our school was having a huge celebration for its twenty-fifth anniversary. The entire school was going to have a balloon launch at the end of the program. My class had already sung their song and now each antsy kindergartener was holding their red, white, or blue balloon, waiting to release it as soon as the band finished playing "America." Sid's blue balloon suddenly floated quietly up into the sky as the rest of the class gasped.

Sid whispered to me, "I just had to set my balloon free."

Before the song was over, half my class was brave enough to set their balloons free, too.

MY HEART BELONGS TO TEACHING

Stolen Torch ☺

Our class was talking about the upcoming summer Olympics in Los Angeles. The children were very excited about watching the opening ceremony, gymnastics, swimming, cycling, and basketball.

Todd added his two cents when he informed the class, "Yeah, some runner grabs the torch from the Statue of Liberty and has to run it all the way to California so they can light the Olympic torch. Then they can start the games."

Kathy's Hat

Kathy looked like she walked right out of a cartoon strip. She was solidly built with straight brown hair, chunky legs, large features, and a deep voice. Kathy had only been around older children and adults before she started school. She was a loveable tomboy who seemed wise beyond her years. This was the early 1960s when most girls wore frilly dresses to school, but Kathy always wore slacks, usually corduroys since jeans were still considered too casual for school. Some of the teachers commented that Kathy looked like she just arrived off a boat from the "old country."

At conference time, Kathy's mother said Kathy hated to wear dresses. She wouldn't even wear one on Easter or Christmas. Her mother wanted Kathy to be more feminine and have some girlfriends. She always played with the boys–pushing and teasing them so they'd notice her and chase her.

One April day, Kathy marched into school wearing an old, oversized dress that she borrowed from her sister, along with dark socks, sturdy black shoes, and on her head was a floppy woman's hat with flowers and a veil. The Annie Hall look had arrived years before the movie! No one had ever worn a hat to school, so everyone came up to Kathy to comment on her hat. Thinking she was getting embarrassed about the attention she was receiving, I asked if she'd like to hang her hat in the closet.

"No," she said. "My mother says a hat always gives a lady a lift."

Kathy wore that crazy hat all day and she received plenty of attention. Girls asked her to play in the doll house so they could observe the hat up close. Boys teased her and she loved it. More excuses to chase them.

Kathy never wore a hat again but she did wear a dress about once every two weeks. Her mother was mystified over the change in Kathy. I guess she had just decided to change her image! For the rest of the school year, she was one of the most popular children with both the boys and the girls.

"B" Words

Chris was a sharp kindergartener with energy to spare. Any assignment the class was given, Chris would turn in double or triple the work.

We were working on the "B" sound one day. The children were asked to look at old catalogs and magazines for ten pictures that started with the "B" sound. Of course, Chris's paper had about twenty-five pictures–front and back. I would write the name of the picture under it as the child watched me and repeated the word. I was speeding along with Chris's paper when I came to a picture I couldn't figure out. I asked Chris was it was.

"Boob," he said.

I nodded my head but didn't say a word or write a label on that picture. Chris had found a bra advertisement and cut out just one cup and pasted it on his page. Let him explain that one to his mother!

My Pal, the Principal

A new boy named Leo arrived in my class. I noticed he was quite a bully with my kids. He was behind in his studies and just didn't seem happy with himself.

After a week or two, I decided I'd better get Leo some help . . . counseling or remedial classes. His records from his former school hadn't arrived yet, so I didn't know what help he had been getting, if any. I quietly asked Leo if he'd ever seen anyone in his old school.

Leo thought for a long while and then answered, "I saw the principal a lot."

Looking Good

My husband, Jerry, and I were looking forward to attending a wedding in Georgetown one fall weekend. I got a ride to work and Jerry was picking me up after school so we could head to the airport. We would be heading to the rehearsal dinner immediately upon landing.

Luckily, my class had music the last hour on Friday. I ran down to the faculty restroom and put on makeup, perfume, high-heeled shoes, my best jewelry, and a beautiful, new, bright silk dress. When I picked up the children from the music room they were impressed at my makeover. One of the boys whistled when he saw me. After we got back to the room and were getting ready for dismissal, Frank touched my elbow and said, "Wow, Mrs. Tryloff, you look like a movie star."

Josie handed me her pencil and notebook and asked, "Can I have your autograph?"

Punish My Foot, Not Me ☺

John was really acting up in class one day. I caught him kicking over a block house that Sarah had built on the floor. I asked him if he needed a time out and he said, "Okay, but the house was in my way!"

When the children got too rambunctious, they would sit in our coatroom for about five minutes. I'd set a timer and also leave the door open so they'd be aware of all the fun they were missing.

A few minutes later, the class was singing as I played the piano. I looked over my shoulder and saw John singing along with the class. He had his head in the classroom and his feet back in the coatroom.

JOANN TRYLOFF

I said, "John, the timer didn't go off yet."
John said, "Mrs. Tryloff, my foot is in the coatroom. That's the part that did the kicking."

Chapter 14

Above and Beyond the Call of Duty

Above and Beyond the Call of Duty

You often hear stories about the money teachers spend out of their own pockets for those little incidentals they just have to have to make a lesson complete. That's so true! Over the years, we do spend hundreds of dollars. In a wealthier district, you have a chance to get reimbursed if you want to take the time to fill out the proper forms. Most often, there just isn't any money available so we become quite resourceful at getting what we want.

We go to garage sales during the summer to get used books for our room's special library. We've come in during our vacation to paint our classrooms or bookcases because our summer maintenance request has been denied for nine years. We buy and decorate t-shirts and sweatshirts to give as special prizes. We sometimes sweet talk our husbands to try to fix a leaky faucet that's been driving us crazy for three years. It's just doing what your heart tells you is appropriate at the moment.

Sometimes you can't stop yourself even if it may get you in trouble. Teachers in this day and age really shouldn't hug a child–let alone kiss him on the head, but of course, if someone needs a hug on a certain day we give them one. We aren't covered under any insurance if we give a child a ride to his grandmother's house without a signed permission slip from one of his parents. "But where are the parents? They were supposed to pick him up an hour ago." The list of rules that restricts teachers is endless. And teachers keep taking chances by bending, and even breaking the rules, hoping the parents and administration will understand if someone complains.

Teachers are so in tune with their children they can sense what a certain child needs most and will try hard to provide some security, assurance, or help. So often, we go above and beyond the call of duty. These are the special "teaching with your heart" moments that give your heart that warm glow. We feel we've made a difference! All we need are a few incidents like these each year and we know we will continue to teach for years to come.

Memories of Mommy

Joey was the sweetest, most sensitive child in my first grade class. He was always kind to everyone and eager to help, but Joey seemed to have a cloud of sadness that hung over him. I never saw him smile, let alone laugh and kid around with the other children. I started to inquire why Joey seemed so sad and I learned he'd lost his mother to cancer the year before.

One day Joey was up at my desk to get some help in math. He carefully laid his hand on top of my head. I looked up at him and giant tears were pooled in his eyes. Before I could say anything, he said, "My mother had soft hair like yours. It smelled pretty like yours, too."

I gave him a hug and whispered, "I bet we both liked the same shampoo or perfume."

That night after school, I checked to see what shampoo I had used and tried to buy that brand every time I ran out. Each day Joey would come to me and stroke my hair two or three times. I hope in some way I was helping him deal with his grief.

MY HEART BELONGS TO TEACHING

Margin Talk

By the time the children got to third grade, they had tests of twelve spelling sentences every week. I always gave them as much time as they wanted to complete the sentences because they were just learning to write in cursive. Of course, the speedy writers and children who had the sentences down pat were finished quickly. I told them they could doodle in the margins while they patiently waited for the others to finish. Thus started a wonderful running dialogue with quite a few of my students.

Harv would write: "Hi Mrs. Tryloff. Tonight's the BIG game! We're the JETS. Score Jets 20, Comets 0."

As I checked his paper, I circled JETS in red and wrote, "Good Luck."

Next Friday, Harv wrote: "We won! Jets 6, Comets 4. Got a new puppy. I want to name it Blacky, but my sister wants to name it Snuggles. Ugh."

Allison, who was normally quite shy, surprised me by writing: "Do you think Ken is nice?"

I wrote back: "I sure do and he's got beautiful eyes."

Next week: "I think I like Ken."

I responded: "I have a feeling he likes you, too. Talk to him today."

She did!

Some children would get out lots of colored pencils and draw beautiful pictures in the margins. Others would ask personal questions, "How long have you been married?" "What's your favorite food?" "Who do you like best in our class?" Then they'd wait patiently until Monday to find out the answers. All they needed was a one- or two-word answer.

The class and I always looked forward to this quiet time before lunch every Friday. It was so nice getting to know some of the children better and reading what they were thinking about during their quiet moments.

JOANN TRYLOFF

Trauma Center

During my break I walked into my friend's kindergarten class. She was hurriedly putting a Superman bandage on Dawn's knee, telling Heather to walk to the office and ask the custodian to come to the room and clean up after Jeff who had just thrown up, and hugging tearful Jimmy who was holding up his finger to show her a sliver he'd gotten from the wooden blocks.

"Welcome to ER," she wearily greeted me. "Where is George Clooney when I need him?"

I Can Do Anything You Can Do ☺

It was the last hour of the day and we were reading together. Everything was nice and quiet when Jean waved her hand and exclaimed, "Mrs. Tryloff, I just pulled my tooth." I took some time with her and said, "You are really growing up. Come to my desk and I'll put your tooth in an envelope so the Tooth Fairy will bring you something tonight." I let her rinse out her mouth and gave her a small hard candy to take the taste out of her mouth.

Back to the reading. A few minutes later, Steve waved his hand and yelled, "I got it out Mrs. Tryloff! I've been wiggling this tooth all day with my tongue and finally I got it!" I stopped and followed the same routine as with Jean.

When I started the story again, I noticed about ten hands in mouths wiggling teeth. Within twenty minutes, we had two more teeth extracted. I couldn't believe it! A record for me. I was really glad to hear the bell ring, putting an end to the tooth pulling contest.

Scratch My Itch

In kindergarten, teachers often are called "mom." At times we are asked to do many of the same things that Mommy does.

I had about three children in line at my desk waiting to get help with their worksheets. When it was Brittany's turn, I noticed she didn't have her worksheet. Before I could ask how I could help her, she turned her back to me and said, "My back is really itchy. Can you please scratch it for me?"

Chapter 15

So Brave, So Sad

Children Are Born Survivors

There are children in every school who have so many responsibilities and worries at home that school is the only place they can relax and enjoy if they can just stay awake. There are young seven-year-old children who scrub floors, warm bottles, change diapers, and prepare food for their brothers and sisters. They are living in trailers and houses with broken windows and no heat, in friends' basements, or even in cars. They've seen their parents die or become mentally ill or live in a drugged fog. They are stealing food from stores for their family and sometimes living on little more than popcorn and water.

Not all of these children are discovered so they can get help from the school or be placed in foster care. I've seen parents who never got out of their drug haze long enough to sign their name to a piece of paper so their child would get a free hot meal at school.

These children have the eyes and souls of adults. They may not know anything about baseball or Barbie dolls, but they do know how to scratch out a survival against horrible odds.

I tried to keep this book upbeat. I wanted to tell you the cute, clever, and wonderful things children come up with. But there is a dark, sad side of life that many children put up with because they love their mothers and fathers and don't realize their life isn't normal.

I'm sure your child has had a school friend whose life was literally hell. His father or stepfather beat him or made him sleep in his own urine because he wet the bed. Maybe his friend's mother spent all her money on alcohol and drugs and left him with little food or supervision in the home for weeks on end.

These children seem to be carrying the weight of the world on their shoulders. They have so many home problems but they try to hide them as they join their happy-go-lucky peers at school every day.

Here are just a few cases of neglect I have run into. You only have to watch the news any day to find many more. Bless these children.

New Bike

Our class was discussing how riding bikes to school was great exercise. Biking was much better than waiting to be picked up by their moms. They could ride with their friends and be home faster than in a car because of all the traffic around school at dismissal time.

I asked how many children had a bike. Poor Jennifer said hers was stolen two months ago. She lived in a trailer park that was well known for trouble: guns, drugs, and fights. She was almost in tears when she told the class that she'd worked and saved all the money she earned plus her allowance for a year and a half to get her new red bike. Her mother helped out by giving her the last thirty dollars for her birthday so she could buy her dream bike.

When I asked if the bike was locked, she said, "Yes, to part of our trailer. But someone cut the lock."

One of the boys said, "You're not too smart. You've got to put it in your garage."

Jennifer said, "We don't have a garage and our trailers are too crowded to bring a bike inside."

Soon after hearing this sad story, I read in the newspaper that Chrysler Corporation was buying bikes to give to needy kids. I made a special point to write Jennifer's story and sent it in.

Lo and behold, the school got a call a month later saying Jennifer was going to receive a bike the next Saturday. There even was a party for the winners and their families.

One month later, Jennifer came into the classroom crying. Sure enough, her new bike had been stolen!

Poor but Proud

There was a family of five who moved into our district in the late fall. They lived in a rented trailer. They had twin kindergarten girls, Sally and Sheila. Sally was assigned to my class. They were obviously very poor and were not getting enough food to eat. Our district tried to help them with free lunches, Christmas baskets, and some clothing. The family would quietly thank us for anything we did for them, but never once did they ask for help.

Spring arrived, and near the end of April, their father came in to me and said they were moving. He gave me a single daffodil and thanked me for all I had done for his daughter, Sally. I told the other kindergarten teacher that I had a feeling we were going to see those girls again. I felt they were leaving our district for some unknown reason and weren't going to be enrolled in any school until the next year.

Just before Halloween the next year, little Sally saw me in the hall and ran to me and hugged me around the legs. I hugged her and said, "Sally, you're back. We missed you so! What happened? Where did you go?"

She said very quietly, "I'm not supposed to tell anyone but we left our trailer and camped in a tent all summer long. Now we've got enough money to rent a trailer for this winter. I'm so glad to see all my friends again."

MY HEART BELONGS TO TEACHING

Time Out for the Wash

There was a time when I tried to help, but actually made life worse for Shawn. I knew Shawn had three younger brothers and sisters at home, plus a young mother who could hardly handle her own life let alone four small children. Shawn would miss school at least one day a week. I was aware of how much Shawn loved school and knew that the free school lunch was often his only meal that day.

His mother had no phone, so one day I brought Shawn up to my desk and asked why he wasn't in school the day before. Shawn avoided my eyes when he answered, "I didn't have any clean clothes to wear."

I was furious with his mother, but you do what you can. When I found out they did have a washer and dryer in their house, I said, "You are a sharp guy. I bet you could do the laundry yourself."

I proceeded to tell Shawn how he could help his mother. I told him how to sort clothes and how much laundry soap to add. I told him to fold the clothes as soon as the dryer turned off. I made Shawn repeat the directions twice to me. As he walked away from my desk, he sighed and his shoulders sagged like an eighty-year-old man.

Shawn didn't miss a day of school for two weeks, but then it started again. When I asked if he was sick, he finally admitted that his mother would keep him home to babysit the others, change their diapers, give them their bottles, and do the wash, while she went out. I was just sick!

Our school got social services in to help Shawn's family, but two months later, they moved. My heart still feels heavy every time I think of young, overburdened Shawn.

Not During Business Hours

Poor Stan lost his breakfast about 10:30 a.m. I helped him clean up and he laid down on our small bed in the teacher's work room. Our school secretary starting calling to ask his mother to pick him up.

At lunchtime, Stan was still asleep in the teacher's room. I checked with our secretary to see if she'd contacted his mother, but she said she'd been calling and got no answer or a busy signal.

One of the older teachers chuckled and said, "I think she's working."

I innocently asked, "What does she do? We don't have a business number for her."

He said, "She hangs out at Arco's Bar and takes noon hour customers back to her room at a motel. I tried to contact her last year about Stan's sister. She must take the phone off the hook during 'business' hours because we didn't get through until 3:00 p.m."

Sure enough, as I walked the children out the door at 3:05 p.m., there was Stan's mother in the office waiting to pick him up.

Doggie Bag

During October, a scrawny little guy with thick glasses was assigned to my first grade class. He looked like he was starving, but I noticed he carried a large sack that appeared to be his lunch. At noon time, I went to the office to ask our secretary, Betty, about Mitch.

"What do you know about Mitch's family? He looked so hungry when he walked into our class. Did you tell his mother about our free lunch program?"

Betty just shook her head, "I offered her the forms to fill out for free lunch as soon as I saw Mitch and his younger brother and sister, but his mother just lowered her eyes and said Mitch will be bringing a sack lunch. That woman is raising three young kids all by herself and just moved here to look for a job. My heart went out to her. She seemed so brave."

During the week as I returned my lunch tray, Mitch was usually still sitting at the first grade table after most of the children left to play on the playground. One noon, I went over to sit with him. I gave him a Hershey bar I had for dessert and talked a few minutes as he ate it. Out of curiosity, I asked, "What did you have for lunch today?"

Mitch proudly answered, "I always make a butter and sugar sandwich. My mother taught me how."

When the bell rang out for the afternoon classes, I noticed Mitch was still carrying his large lunch bag, and it seemed to have more in it than when he arrived in the morning. Most kids just threw their lunch bags away, but I suspected Mitch was using the same one every day.

The next morning, I asked our lunch ladies to keep an eye on Mitch during lunch hour. My suspicion was right. Several children who bought lunch would be in such a rush to get outside that they'd eat only half of their food. Mitch would politely ask if he could have their leftover apples or cookies. Other children who had brought a sack lunch noticed him collecting food and would say,

"Here, you can have my sandwich."

"Do you want a bag of pretzels?"

"How about some carrot sticks? I can't stand them?"

The longer Mitch sat there, the more food he collected to take home for his family to eat at supper time. Poverty had made him very resourceful.

After school that day I completed the forms so Mitch's family could receive food and clothing from County Services. His mother had been too proud to admit they needed help.

Third-Grade Parolee

Ricky arrived in my third-grade class on a Wednesday in November. He was small-boned, short, dirty, and underweight. He had already been to two different schools since September. He, his sister, and his brother were living temporarily with their grandmother. That Friday, a parole officer knocked on my door asking to talk to me about Ricky. He had been involved in several B and Es (breaking and entering) around town. I couldn't believe it! Little Ricky, who looked like a first grader.

I found out his older brother, Craig, who was in the fifth grade, would break a window and put his coat over the window sill so Ricky wouldn't get cut. He'd then boost Ricky up into the house. Ricky would sneak around the house, handing jewelry, video equipment, guns, money, and other valuables to Craig who stuffed them into a pillowcase. If someone came home or woke up, off they'd run. Once in a while, they'd use a bike to escape.

Yes, their parents were aware of what was going on. They were selling the stolen goods and using the money for alcohol and drugs. Poor Ricky, his brother Craig, and younger sister were surviving on any cash they could hide from their parents and used it to buy fast food for themselves

My heart went out to Ricky. He tried hard in school even though it was a struggle to keep up. Soon after Christmas, he was gone. His grandmother just couldn't cope with three undisciplined children. I later heard they were put in a county home because their parents weren't capable of taking care of them. I hoped they weren't split up because they'd tried so hard to stay together and take care of themselves as best they could.

I can only hope those three children have found some happiness in their adult lives.

Too Young for This Tragedy

In the middle of the year, I got a new boy, Gene, who wasn't prepared for third grade. He'd moved many times with his mother, and after two weeks, he was struggling to keep up and he started acting out. Gene did everything to disturb our class and get their attention. He'd make noises, funny faces, throw books and refuse to participate in many activities.

When he'd go to our enrichment classes, he was even more wild and always ended up in the principal's office. The teachers gave up trying to control him.

The worst day was during a blizzard. We were walking back from art class and he opened a door and dashed outside in his t-shirt. I got the class settled and tried to talk him back inside. I finally gave up and called our principal for help. When he showed up I was quietly sitting with a small reading group trying to ignore Gene. He had climbed a snowbank and was banging on our classroom window. We all tried to ignore him but he started throwing snowballs at the window and then started undressing. He just got his shirt off when our principal arrived to take him to the office and calm him down.

Gene was definitely disturbed and had been working with a counselor. His strange behavior was escalating and had finally reached the breaking point. The next morning, Gene came to class rather subdued and quite pale. We soon started our small reading group for those who were having trouble. He sat in a chair with us for two minutes and then got two more chairs and lined them up and laid across the chairs with his arm over his eyes to shut us out. Finally I asked, "What's bothering you, Gene?" He sighed and said, "Oh Mrs. Tryloff, if you only knew."

The group continued reading and I saw a tear slide across his face in frustration.

About five minutes later, Gene's counselor knocked on the door and asked for him. He sulkily got up with his head down and tears falling. I walked with him and asked if I could help. The counselor told him to get his backpack and come with her to the office. As she left, she whispered to me, "Gene won't be back for the remainder of the year. He went down into his basement that morning and saw his mother's boyfriend commit suicide with a shotgun. I'm sure he'll be in a foster home for a while."

We found out Gene had been abused, beaten, and neglected by both adults. We hadn't given him the help he so badly needed.

I felt so bad that Gene had experienced something so terrible at the tender age of nine. For the rest of the school year, I thought of him with sadness and hoped he was finally living in a better place.

Chapter 16

Kisses and Puppy Love

Cupid Strikes Again

Don was all boy! He was never still. Don couldn't wait to get outside for recess so he could run, yell, and play with his boyfriends. His group of friends thought all girls were poison! They wouldn't be caught talking to them, looking at them, or even sitting near them. It was a very macho kindergarten group.

Halloween came and Don was dressed as a devil (what else?) and was running all over the place poking the children with his plastic pitch fork. In walked beautiful, sweet Sheila dressed as a bride in all white with a veil and bouquet. Don stopped short and stared! He walked close to her and followed her all around the room. He brushed off his boyfriends when they asked him to play with trucks. After an hour, he got up the courage and told Sheila, "You are a beautiful bride."

I've never seen cupid work so fast! From that day forward, Don calmed down. He still played with his friends, but when Sheila was in sight, he was at her side. I heard from the children that Don told Sheila he loved her during that first week. The next month, he told me in private that he was going to marry Sheila.

First love is so wonderful! I've always wondered if they might be together today.

MY HEART BELONGS TO TEACHING

The Kiss That Doesn't Count ☺

Every year, I had the children read a fairy tale and then write a script to turn it into a play. The children loved to make the costumes, props, and perform in front of the other third graders. But very often at the end of the play the prince had to kiss the princess before they rode off on a white horse to live happily ever after. The kids giggled like crazy and loved it. But who would be the prince?

Each sex pretended to hate the other. To touch is poison; to kiss, automatic death! Once in a while, a real Romeo would do the deed among five minutes of giggles. Sometimes, a girl would take the role because it gave her lots of lines.

Paul was dying to play the prince role because he was a real ham. He solved the kiss problem by doing it with his eyes closed. He told the kids it didn't count if your eyes were closed. Surprisingly, the children bought it and there were very few giggles. Paul handled the situation like a real pro.

Anything to Be Near My Love

Danny was head over heels in love with Linda. I've never seen such a devoted suitor. Danny got an allowance which he'd save up to buy Linda really expensive gifts. He bought her jewelry, candy, and even a radio. He never spent anything on himself–always something for Linda.

At the end of the school year, the children who had good behavior throughout the year were treated to a movie and snacks by our local theater. Danny was selected to go, but poor Linda had too many detentions and was going to have to stay at school.

Before going on a field trip, the children had to have a signed permission slip from one of their parents. I sent a slip home with Danny in his backpack. After two days, it didn't come back. I sent another and another. Danny kept leaving it in his desk, hiding it, throwing it away, and tearing it up. He just didn't want to go to a movie without Linda, even though he'd earned it. Finally, I realized there wasn't anything I could do. Danny spent the afternoon of the movie in the classroom with Linda, his lady love.

If The Skin Fits

Groups of children were looking through magazines to find pictures of things that started with certain letters. Josh and William lingered over a sunblock ad with a beautiful, long-legged model in a bikini. Josh sighed and said, "Her skin really fits her nice."

William answered, "It sure does!"

Springtime, and a Boy's Heart Turns to Love

Jerry was the class cut-up. He never sat still, finished his work, kept quiet, or stopped showing off. He drove me, and the class, crazy.

Along came spring and as always, it brought romance to my third-grade class. Silly, out-of-control Jerry fell head over heels in love with Tina who was the sweetest, quietest girl in the class. She was very pretty but didn't have boyfriends like the bold girls who chased boys at recess, wrote notes to them during class, and generally flirted with them. I noticed Jerry didn't hit and chase Tina like he did the popular girls. He would stare at her while we read social studies, quickly pick up her pencil if it rolled off her desk, offer to share his science book with her, and try to be near her when we did small group activities. Tina never seemed to realize how Jerry felt about her.

Every Friday, we had a good manners drawing for prizes. The children put their friend's name in a special basket if they had done something nice for them. Of course, Jerry usually had no hope of having his name in that basket. He was the class terror. Then one Friday, there were three prizes and the best one was a Detroit Tiger's opening day towel my husband had gotten at the baseball game. Everyone wanted it–especially the boys. There was also a lovely necklace and a special bag of candies.

Tina's name was drawn first. She had her choice, and I knew she'd take the necklace because she was so feminine. I was wrong! She picked out the Tiger towel that every boy in the class wanted. As she walked to her desk, she nonchalantly dropped the towel on Jerry's desk. He blushed and his whole face lit up as he said "Thank you" so sweetly.

The kids were dumb-founded, and I think pleased by this sweet gesture. They were all smiles and I didn't hear anyone tease either Jerry or Tina about being in love.

That very same afternoon, Jerry's father returned some unfinished papers I'd sent home the night before. He asked if I'd looked at them before they came home. I said I hadn't, and when I looked at them, Tina's name was all over the backs of them with lots of hearts. I just laughed and told him what had happened that afternoon.

For the rest of the year, Jerry was a pleasant child to have around. He tried to please me and worked hard to be good. When he slipped up, he'd quickly glance at Tina to see if she noticed. If only love would have struck in the fall. My class would have been more enjoyable for the whole year!

Older Woman ☺

Kindergartener Ryan confided in me that he liked older women. He said, "My girlfriend is Teresa. She's in the first grade!"

Fall in Love with a Boy!

Overheard while we were in line waiting to see the play "Cinderella": "I can't understand how girls can fall in love with boys. I have two brothers and they're dirty, noisy, smelly, rough, and mean!"

Love Scent ☺

Jessica informed her mother she had a new boyfriend.
"Brian is my boyfriend. I like him because he always smells like peanut butter."

Missing You ☺

Becky whispered to Jean at lunch recess, "Eric likes me."
Jean answered, "What? Are you kidding? He always throws sand at you."
"Yes, I know. But I know he likes me because he always misses."

Romantic Plan

Jodie, one of the cutest girls in my classroom, liked two of the kindergarten boys. They were both vying for her attention during playtime.
Jodie rolled her eyes while talking to her friend Beth. "I'm really in love with John and Bill. What I'm going to do is marry John for a while, and then when I divorce him, I can marry Bill."

Frog Prince

Kristi was a real tough girl who always wore jeans and a t-shirt or sweatshirt to school. She had short, straight hair, a stocky figure and walked around the room with a chip on her shoulder. I felt Kristi wanted to have friends and be considered popular, but she had no idea how to play or share with the other children. She'd approach the girls to play with dolls, but if they gave her a doll to hold, she'd throw it on the floor and say, "Here, take her! She's just a dumb doll."
Next, she'd approach the boys playing with trucks on the floor. She'd grab the biggest one and bulldoze down their block garage.

They'd yell at her and she'd kick their trucks and leave to sulk. She didn't fit in with any group. Eventually, Kristi just stayed on the outside of the groups watching them play. She knew she wasn't welcome. At least she wasn't aggressive any more, but I felt sorry for her because she seemed to want to belong.

In early spring, we started acting out plays. We were working on "The Frog Prince" and started picking children to play the different roles. We'd gotten most of the roles filled and then we came to the Frog Prince. Everyone wanted that part because you got to be in the play a lot and wear the neat green frog costume. All at once, one boy remembered and yelled out, "Ugh, the princess has to kiss the frog!"

No boy would take the part. I finally said, "It doesn't have to be a boy. Would any of you girls like to be the frog? It's a great part!"

From the corner of the group, Kristi shyly raised her hand. Everyone looked at her and she said "I'll try it, Mrs. Tryloff." No one even giggled. They were as surprised as I was that Kristi was actually participating in something.

We had a quick practice and Kristi was doing great. She wasn't embarrassed at all to be dramatic with her lines. She let the princess kiss her sweetly on the cheek. Surprisingly, no one even snickered.

Each day after practice we critiqued our play. The children who didn't have parts offered suggestions on how to improve it and were asked to praise the best performers. Kristi always received the most praise. "Kristi really acts well!" and "I can hear Kristi's lines the best." Kristi just glowed.

She was the star of the play when we presented it to the parents. From the day she volunteered to take the frog's part, the children gradually involved Kristi in their play groups. Kristi mellowed out and was no longer surly or aggressive. By the end of the year, Kristi was one of the most popular children in my class. The Frog Prince had cast his spell on Kristi.

Chapter 17

Reading

Can I Read Yet?

Every few years I'd get a kindergartener who would ask me after the first day or first week of school, "Why haven't you taught me to read yet?"

Everyone had told them, "Just wait until you get to school. You'll learn to read."

It was encouraging that they were so impatient for the process of learning to begin.

What Am I Reading? ☺

Some days in kindergarten, when playtime got too wild and noisy, I'd ask the children to find something they could do silently and then set the timer for ten minutes to give myself a break.

During this quiet time, Sid was sitting on a beanbag chair in the corner looking at a book he'd picked up. As I walked by, I noticed it didn't have many pictures in it. Sid looked at me bewildered and asked, "Can you tell me what I'm reading about?"

MY HEART BELONGS TO TEACHING

So Many Books, So Little Time ☺

The first time I took my kindergarten class into the school library to show them how to check out a book, Louise looked awed as she slowly turned and found she was completely surrounded by books. I heard her whisper to Dawn, "How am I ever going to read all of these? I guess I've got to learn to read real soon."

The Upside Down Club

Finally, it was the last week of school. The children were taking turns reading an interesting story, but the sun was shining, the room was hot, and they were getting antsy. Josh's turn came and he read beautifully. After he finished he said, "See? Upside down!"

Sure enough, he'd read the whole paragraph with his book upside down.

Now everyone had to try it. Surprisingly, any child who was an average or better reader had no problem doing this trick. They had to concentrate a little harder but were happily surprised to find they could do it! Anything to fight boredom!

Different Words ☺

Holly, a first grader, was browsing through the library and kept pulling down a book, looking at the words, and then putting it back on the shelf. I heard her sigh and say to Mary, "I'm never going to learn to read! These words are all different than the ones in our reading books."

Talk a Story

Before we left for home, I often read the children their favorite stories. Each child would get to pick a book they knew or one that looked interesting. When Robert's turn came, he said, "I want you to talk us a story. You know, like a book with no pages."

I was bewildered and said, "What kind of story do you want me to talk about?"

Robert answered, "My favorite is when your brother put a ladder under the bedroom window and at naptime he took the screen out and you climbed out to play instead of napping."

I laughed. The kids loved to hear the wild adventures I had with my brothers and sister. Recalling some of the crazy things I did with my family brought back a lot of memories, and I was thrilled the kids enjoyed the stories so much.

Good Book ☺

The first graders were browsing in the library. They were trying to find two books to check out for book reports. I overheard Cory tell Mark, "It's easy to tell a good book. It's one that has lots of pictures in it."

Teaching Letter Sounds

I was helping the kindergarteners with the "c" sound.
"Brent, what letter do you think 'cat' starts with?"
He shrugged his shoulders.
"C–c–cat. Can you hear the sound at the beginning?"
"I don't know," he replied.
"It's the letter 'c'. Okay. Let's try this word: c-c-car. What does that start with?"
He smiled, "A motor?"

Chapter 18

Random Acts of Kindness

Random Acts of Kindness

As you read in a previous chapter, 'So Brave, So Sad,' no one is aware of what is really going on in a child's home. Children have great empathy toward their peers and even their parents and other adults who are in need. Often, a child will sense his friend is going through some terrible crisis long before an adult does. I've seen many of my children befriend a child who is truly needy. I've also seen numerous random acts of kindness–sharing of lunches, letting a child play with a new doll or just a hug when a child looks ready to break into tears. Children try to help make this old world a better place to live.

Mitten Mystery

When our kindergarten children used the restroom, they had to pass through the coat room. One freezing day, a giggling boy returned from the restroom with a pair of wet, dirty, raggedy socks in his hand. No one would claim them. I quickly took them and put them on our heat register to dry out. I kept sneaking looks at my children's feet, thinking someone couldn't make it to the bathroom in time and had soaked his socks. But everyone had their shoes and socks on. "Just another mystery," I thought.

When we were lining up to go home, Michael was the only one without mittens. It was well below freezing out, and I hated to let him go out in that weather. I told him to keep his hands in the pockets of his hand-me-down summer jacket. As I glanced at his pocket, I saw a piece of the unclaimed sock. I realized that he'd worn the socks as mittens because there were no mittens in his house which he shared with two cousins, three stepbrothers and stepsisters, and two sisters. Michael was taking care of himself as best he could.

The next day, I realized I wasn't the only one who had noticed Michael's pocket. David quietly handed Michael a pair of mittens saying, "Here, I have an extra pair. You can keep these.

Michael couldn't look David in the eye, but he quietly said, "Thank you" and put the mittens in his coat pocket.

Christmas Trades

Every Christmas, we had a gift grab bag. We kept the price between $1.00 and $2.00. I've seen dirty, used Matchbox cars and also $10.00 super gifts that came in all beautifully wrapped. Even in kindergarten, the children do quite well in hiding their disappointment when they receive some "stupid gift" as I've heard them called.

I've seen many acts of kindness after the gift exchange. Bonnie opened a small, slightly used stuffed animal. Her friend, Julie, unwrapped twelve brightly colored bangle bracelets, plus a fashion doll like Barbie. Julie took one look at Bonnie's face and quickly said, "I've got so many of these bracelets. What colors do you like?" They each put on six bracelets and played together until we ate our treats. What a special friend!

There have been some super trades. When Sean, who hated to read, received a great book about dinosaurs, he thumped it on his table and looked really displeased. Nearby, Paul had gotten a Matchbox car. He was my class bookworm. When he noticed the gift Sean had opened, he walked over and asked if he could look at the book. Paul said, "Sure! Take it!"

Paul ran back to his table and got his car. "Here," he said, "would it be all right to trade?"

"Great!" exclaimed Paul, as he zoomed off with his prized car.

Sometimes life turns out okay after all.

Miss You Already

Andrew was just starting kindergarten. His father walked him to school the first morning, hugged him, and said, "Gee Andrew, I'll really miss you today while you're at school. I can't believe you're old enough to go to school. Be good. I'll miss you."

Andrew looked concerned and then said, "Don't worry, Dad. I'll be home when you get out of work. You can see me then."

Reading Tutors

Kids love to help out and are always willing to lend a hand if you are willing to trust them with a task and are thoughtful enough to praise and thank them for a job well done.

Samantha could not read anything on a third-grade level. She tried hard, but was discouraged when she discovered she could figure out only half of the words. She never wanted to read to the class. All the children were embarrassed for her, too. Finally, I found a series of books with interesting stories which were at Samantha's reading level.

We all decided to help Samantha learn all the words so she would be able to read the whole book to the class. Everyone wanted to help her. Every day, Samantha chose one person to read with her. They were so into the project that I often found the helper spending all his or her time with Samantha and her book.

When Samantha was ready to read her first book, she was very proud. She sat in our special reader chair and read the whole book without one mistake. The children had held their breath while Samantha read, and when she finished, they started clapping wildly.

From then on, Samantha's reading picked up. She read all the fifteen books in the series. The children fought to be the one to help Samantha each day. They each felt they were responsible for Samantha's improvement, and I'm sure they were. Learning from her peers made the breakthrough for Samantha that four different teachers were unable to accomplish.

Wheelchair Wheelies

One winter morning, I fell down the stairs at my home and broke my leg. But I was back in school the next day with a cast and crutches.

Getting around the school building on crutches took forever and left me exhausted. Every day, I seemed to walk miles with the children to their special classes, lunch, buses, and offices. It took me a few days to realize I needed a wheelchair to move around more easily.

Once I got the chair, the children thought it was an honor to push me between classes. They took such good care of me. They wouldn't let me get a thing on my own . . . water, chalk, papers, books, and lunch were all brought quickly to my desk. The children were so observant and great about anticipating my every need. At one point, I thought one of the girls was going to come right into the restroom with me.

The girls pushed me so slowly and carefully that I thought we'd never get to our special class on time. With the boys, it was a different matter. They would zoom my wheelchair down the halls so quickly my hair would be streaming straight out behind me. They thought the wheelchair was a race car! As we'd approach a corner, I'd yell, "Whoa!" I was afraid they'd turn too soon and I'd bump my cast into the wall.

I was definitely glad when I got back on my own two feet and out of that race car wheelchair.

Chapter 19

It Was All Worth It

Compliments

Some of the nicest compliments I ever received were when a parent told me how much a child's personality had blossomed during a year in my class. I loved to hear that a child would look forward to coming to school and he'd begin to talk about his school projects and all the friends he'd met. It made me feel great when I saw a student lose his shyness and become more outgoing and confident during his stay with me. I really felt that if a child was happy and confident with himself, learning would come easily. Most children are open to new experiences when they are presented in an interesting, exciting way.

Gifts from the Heart

The best gifts I received from my students were simply gifts from the heart. Children have no inhibitions. If they like you, they'll do anything to please you and try to make you happy. These gifts weren't received at Christmas or bought by the student's parents, but would appear any old day and lift my spirits for weeks.

I've been given many of the kids favorite stuffed animals because we were reading a story about a puppy or I'd mentioned that I collected bunnies.

If I happened to mention that I thought the rock Jimmy brought in for sharing was really unusual, he'd say, "You can keep it," even though I knew Jimmy carried it around as a good luck piece.

I'd say, "That's a beautiful, big tooth you've got there!" as someone handed me the tooth they'd just pulled out.

They'd ask, "Do you want to keep it?"

Then there was Danny who said, "You can keep it, Mrs. Tryloff. I only get ten cents from the tooth fairy."

Bouquets from the Heart

In the spring, I loved the bouquets that were handpicked by the children on their walk to school. I've been given a handful of cherry blossoms that Steve jumped up and pulled off a branch that hung over the sidewalk. I had to float them in a pan of water for everyone to admire.

I was given only the heads of about seven tulips. I had a feeling some neighbor would be mad when they discovered those missing blooms.

Best of all were the wild flowers my boys would bring in, roots and all. They'd pick them as they took a shortcut across an empty lot. We'd all check out how long the roots had to be to get nourishment and hold the plant in the ground. If I was really ambitious, we'd try to find the names of the flowers in a wild flower book I kept at school.

One Monday, I got a lovely bouquet of long-stemmed roses and baby's breath. They were a little wilted but still gorgeous. When I thanked Sandy for the roses she confided, "My mother received them from her boyfriend. They had a fight this weekend and my mother didn't want the roses in the house anymore."

We all enjoyed the second-hand roses!

And then there were the fuzz-balls—dandelions gone to seed! By the time these bouquets were handed to me, most of the fuzz was floating all over the room. The children loved to huff and puff and blow the fuzzy seeds all across the floor.

Marry Me

Sean was in my very first kindergarten class. It was love at first sight for both of us. He would follow me around like a little puppy and hang on my every word. Sean was always under foot waiting to help clean the paint brushes, takes notes to the office, or shut the windows. He told his parents he loved me and wanted to marry me.

His mother was a wonderful woman. Some mothers get upset and get jealous of their child's first teacher. Mrs. Ryan just laughed and said she hoped Sean would find someone as nice as me when the time came for him to marry.

About thirty years later, I ran into Mr. and Mrs. Ryan. They recognized me and laughed as they told me Sean was still in love with "me." He had married a wonderful woman who was a teacher, and even looked quite a bit like me.

The Ryans had ten children and I had taught many of them. With all those children and their many teachers through the years, they still remembered me! All teachers love to hear from and about their former students. It made me feel great. You see the world through rose-colored glasses for days.

Share my Teacher

Jodie's mother stayed a few minutes after she'd walked Jodie to school. She pulled me aside and laughed as she said, "Last night Jodie said she liked you so much but she was mad because she had to share you with all her classmates. She even said it would be nice if you could be her mom! I should be jealous, but I can handle it."

What a great compliment!

Love Flashcards

My kids had been terrible this particular week and I was glad I had to attend an all-day offsite workshop. When I returned the next day, my children were so happy to see me. Their substitute had been strict and wouldn't allow the children out of their seats for anything…. "Not even the bathroom, Mrs. Tryloff!"

Jim, who had been a handful that week, silently held up a homemade sign during roll call. The sign said "I love you, Mrs. Tryloff." Later that day, I snuck over to him and quietly told him how good that sign made me feel.

The rest of the year, whenever another child was giving me trouble or when Jim sensed I was feeling low, he would quickly write, "I love you, Mrs. Tryloff" on the back of a worksheet and silently flash it for me to see. Jim was one of the biggest and oldest boys in my class, but was also very sensitive. Whenever I saw his special sign, I glowed all day.

Time and Time Again

One day, a father praised me up and down because his son was finally able to tell time. He said he'd worked with George for hours in both first and second grade but he couldn't catch on. I explained that George was just ready now that he was in third grade. Everything fell into place and started to make sense.

That bit of praise really made my day and made me realize my teaching was making a difference.

Miracle Workers

Dennis was a sweet guy in my kindergarten class, but as the weeks went by, I realized there was something wrong. His speech was mixed up. His sentences were very short—two or three words. You could figure out most of the words, but a lot of the sounds were garbled and strange sounding. Within two weeks, I placed Dennis in speech class, but it didn't seem to help. Often, Dennis would grunt out words and I had to ask him to repeat his questions. He wasn't responding to my directions and would ignore the cleanup time bell.

I kept going back to my friend, Betty, who was the speech teacher, asking for help. I didn't feel Dennis was as slow as he appeared and I didn't want him placed in a special education class.

Finally, Betty got an audiometer–a machine that tests hearing. She'd never used one before, so she tested Dennis again and again. Betty thought the audiometer might be defective because Dennis was having a hard time responding. At last, we asked his family to have his hearing checked by a specialist.

The day Dennis's hearing was checked, his mother was at our door when we let the children go home. She thought we were miracle workers! She was in tears as she confessed she often thought Dennis had a severe disability but hadn't confided her fear to anyone. She was so embarrassed that in five years she hadn't realized Dennis was nearly deaf. Betty and I were just as embarrassed because we hadn't immediately recognized his disability.

Dennis was fitted for hearing aids for both ears and graduated with honors twelve years later.

Make My Day

During a Friday spelling test, I caught Traci handing Diane a note. I took it from them and gave them one of my sternest looks. At lunch time, I saw the note laying on my desk and decided to read it while I munched my lunch.

"I love Mrs. Tryloff's hair. I wish mine was long and swingy like hers."

"Me too. And her outfit is cool today. She is the nicest teacher ever!"

Their compliments made my day, and I felt badly about embarrassing them in class.

IOU

At lunch time, Matthew came up to my desk to pay back the quarter I loaned him to buy lunch the week before. He winked as he slid a Hershey bar on my desk along with the quarter.

"For interest," he said.

What a doll! I hadn't expected to see the quarter again, let alone the sweet surprise.

Play Tickets

It's always an honor to be remembered many years later by one of your former students.

Sarah was an outgoing, bright, and beautiful girl who had been in one of my kindergarten classes. Twelve years later, she had the lead in our high school play, "Carousel." One spring day, she knocked on my kindergarten door to say "hello" and hand me two tickets for the play on Saturday. What a treat to see Sarah! She said she always remembered her great kindergarten year and all those crazy, impromptu plays we put on for the other classes.

I've been watching for your name, Sarah, starring in a Broadway play or movie. "Break a leg!"

Another former student came in to see me and handed me two tickets to see the play he was in at Michigan State. Ken remembered all through the years that I'd graduated from MSU. He thought it would be fun for me to visit the campus and see their new theater.

Of course, I went and even visited backstage with all the actors in "Tommy." What a thrill.

Chapter 20

Looking Back—It Was Wonderful!

Early Elementary Fears

During my thirty-one-year career, I taught approximately 1,000 children. Over these years, children have always worried about the same things. Here are the top twenty fears that most children have on their minds:

1. Someone they think is really cool won't be their friend.
2. Parents are always fighting.
3. Everyone in the class considers them a "dork" or "nerd."
4. Parents may divorce.
5. Being bullied by older/bigger kids.
6. Dad or Mom will lose their job.
7. No one will be there when they get home.
8. Nightmares or monsters in their bedroom.
9. Mom or Dad will hit them for bad grades or something they've done wrong.
10. Being too short.
11. Being too fat.
12. One of their parents will die because they smoke cigarettes.

13. Stranger danger
14. Dad won't come pick them up for the weekend (if parents are divorced).
15. They will get lost in a crowd or large area.
16. Mom or Dad will get sick or hurt.
17. Someone will offer them drugs and they won't know what to do.
18. Mom or Dad loves their brother or sister more than they love them.
19. All the bad news they see and hear on TV might happen to their family.
20. Guns.

I Love Kids Because . . .

- ♥ They give me a hug and then race out the door on the last day of school screaming their lungs out, "School's out! School's out! Teacher let the fools out. No more books, no more teacher's dirty looks. Freedom!"
  The next morning, as I open all the classroom windows to air out the room while I clean up there are four or five bikes outside and kids sticking their heads in the windows. "Do you need any help, Mrs. Tryloff? I can wash the desks. Can I carry those books for you?"
- ♥ Shawna hands me a tulip head she snitched from her neighbor's front yard and says, "I found the first flower of spring just for you Mrs. Tryloff."
- ♥ When they have to go, they have to go! Marty waves his hands at me as he dashes to the bathroom yelling, "I got to go pee!"
- ♥ They tell the truth even though they might suffer the consequences. . .
    - ♥ "Yes, I copied Joan's answers. She is really smart."
    - ♥ "I took her Tootsie Pop because she's on a diet."

- ♥ "I didn't mean to push him down. He was walking too slowly."
- ♥ "I know I'm late. My mother had a new boyfriend spend the night and she cooked us a fancy breakfast this morning to impress him."
- ♥ "Yes, I have Sharon's quarter. It rolled under my desk so I thought it's mine now."
- ♥ The sweet kisses and hugs some of the children gave me as they left for home every day.

Tricks of the Trade

Over the years, I've really come to admire the parents of my students. They gave up a lot to raise such great kids. Many times, I couldn't figure out how they could have so many responsibilities and remain sane. Here are some parenting tricks that were shared with me.

- ♥ Mrs. Kidler had five children in seven years, and I taught all of them in kindergarten. By the time Dave, her middle child, appeared in my class, I had to compliment her on how neat and coordinated her children's clothes always were.
  She laughed and said, "Every night I lay out each child's outfit and they are all basically one color. Today's color was navy. As soon as they go to bed, I scoop up all their dirty clothes and wash them in one load. Of course, a lot of their underwear ends up matching, too."
- ♥ Mrs. Bates had twelve children and I taught most of them in kindergarten. Every child was sharp as could be with wonderful manners and a very caring attitude. The Bates' were concerned about their children's education. If I asked them to help Becky with her counting for ten minutes each day, they'd be sure she was tutored for twenty minutes.

When Mrs. Bates came to pick up her children, she was always dressed so nice; her long hair and makeup were perfect and she seemed so stress free.

When I asked what her secret was, she said, "The children really aren't any trouble. Getting to school on time goes smoothly because the older children help out. When they make their lunches, they make one or two more for the younger ones. They help dress them and comb, braid, and curl hair. We turn off the television for two hours each night while the children help each other with homework. Everyone has their specialty–some are good in reading, others are great in math. They all have many chores. Plus Harold, my husband, is easygoing and isn't afraid to help around the house."

To this day, the Bates family is still my ideal family.

♥ Mrs. Egan was another exceptional example. She was a single mother raising three children on her own, working two jobs to make ends meet. She was always in a rush, disheveled, a loving airhead. Never once did she neglect her children. Even though she had no time to bake or had money for extras, she found a way to send in treats to her children's classes by shopping "day old" bakery treats at the grocery store.

Here are a few more creative ideas and solutions I've received from parents:

- ♥ Use rinsed out soup cans or Styrofoam cups for paint class. No clean up–just throw away after class.
- ♥ Forget about fussy paint aprons–have children bring in old t-shirts. No buttons or ties to worry about, just slip the shirt over their heads.
- ♥ Use clotheslines and clothespins to dry and display wet paintings.
- ♥ Boots won't slide on? Pull plastic bags over the shoes first.

- ♥ Need wings and halos for the Christmas play? Use wired star tinsel to bend into the proper shapes.
- ♥ Bless my children's parents . . . they were the real angels!

Magic Moments

- ♥ The anticipation of meeting my new class for the year. I'd be waiting for the bell to ring as I looked around my spotless and brightly decorated room. I couldn't wait to have it messed up with paints, paste, mud, and smudges.
- ♥ The perfect fall day to take my kindergarteners for a walk in the nearby park to gather leaves and look for signs of fall. I'd pretend to be lost and asked if anyone remembered the way back to school. A couple brave explorers triumphantly led us back safely.
- ♥ John's face lighting up as he read his paragraph to the class for the first time without making one mistake. The whole reading group clapped. They were happy for John, too.
- ♥ When a child brought in two birthday treats for me. "In case you get really hungry" or "One for Mr. Tryloff, too."
- ♥ A snowy, freezing morning in the middle of January–giant snowflakes swirling outside the wall of windows near my desk. My children were quietly reading, nice and snug in our warm classroom. Who could ask for more? All was well in the world.
- ♥ A bouquet of dandelions or wild flowers picked just for me on the way to school.

Children Returning to School

One of the happy surprises of teaching was having your former students stop in to see you when they were in high school or college. Near the end of my career, I taught children (and sometimes grandchildren) of my former students. They'd walk in the room and be shocked to see a computer in the corner. They'd often say, "This room used to be so much bigger."

I'd just laugh and tell them, "You've gotten so much bigger."

One day when I returned from a workshop, I picked up my substitute report and found it was signed by one of my former kindergarten students, Mary Johnson. She had written a personal note and attached it to the form–"Thanks for encouraging me and being my role model."

I caught up with Mary the next time she was in the building. She had just gotten engaged and was radiant with happiness. I wished her luck in finding a job and much happiness with her new husband. Seeing Mary made me glow for the rest of the day.

Mark had been a hyper, comical class clown in kindergarten. Smart and loveable, but a real handful. I was walking down the hall toward my room one morning when I heard a man's voice call out, "Hey, Mrs. Tryloff."

Sure enough, it was Mark Bronston. I saw he hadn't changed a bit as he pedaled down the hall on a unicycle. He was now a fireman and had just brought his young son, Randy, to our headstart program. He really wanted Randy to be in my kindergarten class the next year.

"He's just like me Mrs. Tryloff. Brace yourself!"

High schoolers would wander through my room at Open House and ask if the witch's broom still came to my classroom at Halloween. They'd often go to their exact desk and try to sit in it. I've seen them open a certain cupboard to see if the puzzles were still there. They'd lean way over to take a drink from our low water fountain and then say, "The water still tastes the same."

Six-foot-tall seniors would run their fingers along the chalkboard ledge and study the alphabet and number charts on the walls. Often someone would comment on how tall the tree outside the window had gotten. They'd ask if I still took the kids out to read under the tree on hot days or if we still had hula-hoop beanbag races.

Some of the visitors could remember the names of all the children who sat near them. And some could even recite the names of all the children who were in their class so many years before.

As I talked to these former students, I always hoped that their memories were happy ones. Childhood is so fleeting and I wanted them to have wonderful school memories.

Farewell

Teaching kept me young. The children had such a high-energy level and my classrooms were brimming over with their inquisitiveness, exuberance, innocence, truthfulness, impatience, selfishness, anxiousness, awkwardness, vivaciousness, and frankness. I always loved the thrill of trying to keep one step ahead of them and channeling their enthusiasm toward learning.

I finally felt grown up when I sent away for my retirement papers. The day they arrived, I felt mature and proud of my accomplishments, yet sad to leave those wonderful children.

Just like Peter Pan, I didn't want to leave Never Land.

About the Author

JoAnn Tryloff always loved children and wanted to teach from an early age. She graduated with a degree in education from Michigan State University and taught in California and Michigan for thirty-one years. She was delighted to be with her students watching them grow and mature as they learned.

When she retired from teaching, she spent two years recalling memories of her students. This book includes some of the more memorable moments.

JoAnn stays active biking and skiing and travels extensively. She currently lives with her husband in Waterford, Michigan.

CPSIA information can be obtained
at www.ICGtesting.com
Printed in the USA
LVHW01s0605130218
566352LV00006B/9/P